# *Relive*
# INDIRA
# GOSWAMI

## The Rich Legacy Of Her Stories

# *Relive* INDIRA GOSWAMI

## The Rich Legacy Of Her Stories

Translated by
Gayatri Bhattacharyya

Vitasta

*Let Knowledge Spread*

Published by
Renu Kaul Verma
Vitasta Publishing Pvt Ltd
2/15, Ansari Road, Daryaganj,
New Delhi - 110 002
info@vitastapublishing.com

ISBN: 978-93-82711-41-4
© South East Asia Ramayana Research Centre, 2014

Typeset & Cover Design by Vitasta Publishing Pvt Ltd
Printed by Vits Press, New Delhi

The highest literary award Jnanpith winner, late Dr Indira Goswami (Mamoni Raisom Goswami) is undoubtedly one of the brightest Assamese literary scholars. She earned a niche for herself at both national and international levels. She spoke out boldly and with passion about those whose voices have been silenced or never heard — women, the marginalised, the powerless, the unfortunates.

As a scholar, an academic, a translator, poet, novelist and activist, she brought passion, belief and dedication to all that she did.

Dr Goswami wrote more than 26 novels and hundreds of short stories which have been translated into many languages. She won numerous awards and honours for her writings such as the Sahitya Akademi Award, the Kamal Kumari Foundation National Award, the Bharat Nirman Award, the Katha National Award. She was conferred the Principal Prince Claus award — a major honour for a unique writer and activist, and was awarded the Asom Ratna posthumously by the Government of Assam.

*The word 'barsati' 4 appear in multiple idover*

# Content

*Groswami Language incorporates Romanticism. V chhayavad too.*

*Rashtra bhasha Examinations — Research.*

# Publisher's Note

For some people in this world, their lives don't end with their death. Indira Goswami is one among them. Her writings have immortalized her and we at Vitasta wanted to revisit her through her soul-touching writings. We believe that the future generations need to read all that she wrote, for her novels and short stories serve as the real mirror of the society that we live in.

In our endeavour, we came in touch with Savita Sarma who is Indira Goswami's younger sister and executive president of the South East Asia Ramayana Research Centre. The stories are translated by Gayatri Bhattacharyya and the process of translation started with efforts from Alaka Goswami and Geetali Baruah. The stories are edited by Veena Batra.

This book tells us stories that move with unexpected twists and turns and catch the reader unawares at the end filling him with awe, sometimes shock and horror.

We hope all readers, young and old, will enjoy this rare collection of short stories from Indira Goswami's treasure box. For the first time, these stories have been translated from Assamese. Through this book, we sincerely hope that readers will relive the legacy of her masterly art of storytelling.

# PURIFICATION "SANSKAAR"

Pitambor, the merchant, sat dejectedly in front of his house. He still had not taken off his mud plastered shoes. Indeed he had a weakness for his pair of old leather shoes. At one time Pitambor had been a healthy and well- built man. Now he was about sixty years old, and although that was not an age that could be said to be 'old' for a man, all kinds of worries and discontentment weighed him down, and these had taken their toll. His face sagged, and he had a haggard look about him. His head was always downcast; he could never look directly at the person he was talking to. The way his head invariably hung down, it seemed as though he was scrutinizing the ground, searching intently for something!

A big teak tree had been recently cut down, and Pitambor sat on the stump looking at the children with their improvised fishing rods, trying their luck in the gutters that lined both sides of the road. The incessant rains of the last few days had made the entire village muddy and slushy. The sides of the *kutcha* road had become covered with all kinds of vegetation, both edible and useless, and the frogs were having a great time jumping from one gutter to the other.

Pitambor was looking intently at one particular boy who was trying to untangle his fishing line from an arum plant, when a deep voice suddenly caught his attention. He looked up to see the priest, Krishnakanta, standing near him. "Pitambor,"he said, "you have been sitting there engrossed in those children for a long time. You were sitting exactly like this when I passed by some time ago, and you are still sitting in the same place in exactly the same way — staring intently and with a peculiar longing at those children. Is it because you do not have any children of your own? 'Whose beloved child is being chased to the waters? Call out and bring him back so that I can kiss him!' — Is that what you are thinking? By the way, is your wife any better? Is she able to leave her bed and do some work now?"

"No. How can she move about? Her hands and feet have become swollen. I have already taken her to the hospital in Guwahati at least twenty times, but she is no better."

"There seems to be no chance of your ever having any children of your own then? So your family will become extinct," said the mischievous and malicious priest.

Pitambor sighed in dejection. What else could he do? Krishnakanta stood there silently for a while. He was dressed in a knee length old *dhoti*, a tattered and worn out kurta, and an equally old *endi chaddar*. His cheeks were hollowed as he had only the two front teeth left — all the others had fallen out so that when he spoke, his face took on an odd and twisted shape! His eyes had a malicious and sly look, and his balding pate only intensified his cunning look. He came near Pitambor and whispered, "Have you given any thought to what you will do if something happens to your wife? Have you thought about marrying again?"

Pitambor was about to answer when he happened to look up and his eyes fell on Damayanti. She was the widow of the priest Shambhu, who had died not too long back. Everyone knew that she was a woman of loose character, and after her husband died, she had become the centre of attraction for all the young men of the village.

Krishnakanta called out to her, "Where are you coming from, Damayanti?" he asked.

"Where do you think I am coming from?" she replied. "Don't you see the *endi* silk worms in my hands?"

"So you have started hobnobbing with that Marwari businessman, have you?"

Damayanti did not reply, and instead started to squeeze out the water from the bottom end of her soaking wet *mekhela*. As she bent down to do so, her blouse rode up from her waist to her breast exposing her slim, soft and fair waist. Neither men could resist looking at this attractive spectacle, but the priest quickly averted his gaze. After she had squeezed out the water, she calmly walked away without even bothering to look towards the two men.

"They say that she has no inhibitions and even eats fish and meat," said Pitambor. "Yes, I heard that too," replied Krishnakanta. "She has put all the Brahmins to shame. She does, and eats, whatever she likes, and does not care for any traditions or rules. In the beginning, after Shambhu died, when she cooked fish for her two daughters, she used to go down to the river and bathe and then cook separately for herself. But now, I am told, she does not bother, and even sits with the girls and eat the fish."

"Yes," replied Pitambor. "I have seen her taking fish from the fishmonger woman in exchange for paddy."

"Dear me!" ejaculated Krishnakanta. "What is the world coming to! A widow buying two fish in exchange for a bit of paddy!"

"Softly, *Purohit*, softly," said Pitambor. "You do not need to publicize the fact that a Brahmin widow is eating fish. Such things are common these days, even in orthodox places like Dakhinpaar and Uttarpaar. And I do not really think it is such a sin. These rules of yore should be abolished."

Staring at the departing figure of Damayanti for some time, Pitambor asked, "Bapu, what is the condition of your clients these days? Has it changed at all?"

"What a surprising question, Pitambor! You know everything and yet pretend not to know! Don't you know that it is because of the quarrel between my brother and myself over our clients that I am in this poverty-stricken condition?"

"It is mainly because your brother went around telling everyone that you do not know how to read Sanskrit," replied Pitambor.

Krishnakanta jumped up in anger. "Tell me," he shouted, "how many priests are there these days who can recite the *mantras* as clearly and correctly as Narahari Bhagabati? We studied at the *tol*, the school for priests, together. He was the one who got the caning, not me. No, no! The main reason for our poverty-stricken condition is the attitude of the clients — of those people who ask us to go and conduct their *pujas* for them. We priests who know how to conduct the rituals and *pujas* should not have been in such impoverished conditions. In the olden days, there was no problem getting at least one sacred thread, a pair of *dhotis*, and some money from each of our clients every month. But nowadays everything is different. The people want to perform the rites and *pujas* but are unwilling to pay the priests. Only the other day, one of our oldest clients, Mahikanta Sarma's two sons were taken to Kamakhya temple for their '*upanayan*' ceremony. One of my clients in Maisanpur, Surja Sarma, held the *shraddha* ceremonies of his mother and father together on the same day. People are gradually starting to ignore the Nandimukh *Shraddha*, the *shraddha* ceremony of nine ancestors, so essential a part of the wedding ceremony. And of course the smaller rituals and *pujas*, like the naming ceremony, home blessing, Basanti Puja, purifying a house by holding a '*hom*', a purifying and sanctifying holy fire if a vulture happened to roost on it, etc., have become things of the past. Time was when a man had to undergo a purifying ritual if he lost his sacred thread. But how many Brahmin boys today even chant the Gayatri *mantra*!"

Pitambor had been listening to the priest's lecture without saying a word. His mind was still on Damayanti, and her lovely silky smooth back exposed when she bent over to squeeze the water from her soaking wet *mekhela*. He thought that he had never seen such a beautiful woman's back before! And it was not as though he had not seen or touched a woman's body before. He had married his second wife just two months after his first wife had died, mainly because his first wife had died childless. But this second wife was a sick woman. Soon, she became almost completely bed-ridden due to acute rheumatism. Pitambor had taken her to doctors in Guwahati many times, but to no avail. Ultimately the woman had become thin, more like a skeleton than a living woman! She lay in her bed all day, quietly watching her husband's behaviour. The man seemed to have almost lost his senses longing for a son to carry on his family name! People said that he was waiting impatiently for his sick wife to die. After a few years he had given up going to the hospitals in Guwahati, and had given up all hope for a son and heir. He was so anxious to have a son that nothing else interested him. The priest was in front of him lamenting his lot in life, but Pitambor hardly heard him. His wife had signalled to one of the servants from her bed to go and get a '*morha*', a cane stool, for the priest to sit on, but Pitambor was not even aware of when the servant had come and gone!

"You are so absent minded, engrossed all the time with only the fact that you don't have a son and heir, that many people here in our '*satra*' have started saying that you are becoming unbalanced and that you are on the verge of insanity," said Krishnakanta. "There are hundreds of people in the world who do not have any children. It is nothing so terrible. And why don't you think of what our gurus have said — that families, sons etc. are after all transitory things, and hence valueless — simply manifestations of '*maya*'."

Pitambor simply lowered his head in dejection. The priest noticed that his hair was greying, that his eyes were circled with small cobweb like wrinkles. The man had become completely unmindful of how he dressed, and his shoes were caked with layers of mud.

Krishnakanta was overwhelmed by a sense of pity and compassion for Pitambor. Just a few years back, the older citizens had called him the '*gora* soldier' because he was so well built, fair, and healthy. There was no dearth of money or means, but the poor man had no peace of mind. His granary was full, but there was no one to enjoy it! Suddenly Krishnakanta said something almost unheard of! But before saying it he looked all round to check that there was no one nearby. But the door of Pitambor's bedroom was wide open, and he could see the skeleton like body of Pitambor's wife lying on the bed. Her sharp eyes, he saw, were shining with a peculiar brightness as though she was trying to find out what the priest was saying to her husband. Krishnakanta was shocked to see that a single glance, even from a distance, could be so keen, and could express such heartfelt sadness. Even so, he whispered to Pitambor, "If you think that you can help me with some money, I too will help you to get what you so desire."

"How?" asked Pitambor. "How will you arrange things?"

"Don't worry about the arrangements. There will be no problems."

"What do you mean?"

"What I mean is that I will arrange matters so that when you meet her, there will be no question of her not conceiving.

I have found out that she has aborted and buried the results of her illicit and guilty pregnancies four times!"

Pitambor almost shouted, "Bapu, are you talking about Damayanti?"

"Yes, yes. I am talking about Damayanti," replied the priest. Our Brahmin girls have started going across the Dhaneswari River to marry Sudra boys. Don't you know that the Gosain of Mukteswar *satra's* son has gone and married a Muslim girl? It seems that our Gandhi Maharaj has shown this path— that caste and community do not matter. That is why I am thinking about this matter of Damayanti for you."

Pitambor jumped up in excitement. "What matter are you talking about?"

"If you so desire, you can make Damayanti your own woman." Krishnakanta glanced towards the open bedroom again. The eyes of the woman lying on the bed were wide open, and it seemed as though they were burning with a fierce fire. She was staring at him!

Pitambor ran and tried to clutch the priest's hands, but the latter hastily stepped away. He had just bathed and was on his way to the Adhikaar's house. He had been asked to bathe the idol of Murulidhar in the Adhikaar's temple because the regular priest there had gone to Guwahati. It was a very important duty and he had to be clean and untouched by any other person, particularly one who was not a Brahmin. But the priest's words had opened an unthinkable world for Pitambor, and he did not know how to thank the man.

"So Pitambor," said Krishnakanta, "It seems that you have

been thinking about this for some time?"

A happy smile played over Pitambor's lips! Once again Krishnakanta glanced towards the bedroom. The woman's eyes were now shut, but it seemed as though she was undergoing some terrible suffering and pain. Touching the priest's feet Pitambor spoke humbly and pleaded, "Bapu, do this for me. Everyone knows that she goes out at night to bury the things she aborts. I know it too. But she is a Brahmin woman and I am a Sudra. If she comes to me I will place her on a pedestal and worship her."

A sly and crooked smile spread across Krishnakanta's toothless mouth. "It will not be easy. I will have to negotiate. I will have to make the two girls agree to it and for that I will have to bribe them with sweets from your shop."

Pitambor got up hurriedly and went inside. The eyes of the woman lying on the bed flew open. She had probably just shut her eyes and was not asleep. She saw her husband go to the small wooden box that was placed on top of a stool and open it and she also saw him going out to Krishnakanta again after a while.

"You will let me know everything soon, won't you?" he said to the priest.

Taking the twenty rupees from the *Mahajan*, the wily priest went away with a mischievous smile.

Seven days passed without any word from him, while Pitambor waited eagerly every day. He had seen Damayanti a number of times making her way to and from the 'adhikaars' house to deliver the sacred threads she spun from the finest cotton. It was only now that he looked at her properly and discovered that he had never seen a woman as beautiful as her!

Her mother they said was from the village of Routa situated on the banks of the Dhansri river. And after seeing Damayanti now, Pitambor came to the conclusion that the Brahmin girls from near the Dhansri river must be among the most beautiful women in the whole country! Her father, the priest Purnananda, had once lost a couple of his ploughing bullocks, and at that time he had many clients in comparatively distant places like Maisanpur, Gargora etc. Searching for his precious bullocks, Purnanda had gone to the village of Routa on the Dhansri river side. No one seemed to know why he had gone so far to find his cows. But it was then that he saw and married the beautiful daughter of Bhagawati of Routa village. No priest of the area had ever before married a girl from so far away!

It was the month of June, and the rivers and wet lands were overflowing with water. Both sides of the *kutcha* road were full of the shrubs and climbing plants that invariably come with the season. The road running in front of Pitambor's house had become covered with mud and slush. But in spite of the muddy and slippery road, Pitambor saw Damayanti walking along plucking the edible greens like the tasty 'kolmou' which grew in abundance on the roadsides in the wet weather. She had lifted her *mekhela* up to her knees, and was accompanied by her six year old daughter, who was completely naked. Damayanti's legs and hands were soft and shiny, and healthy, like a new mango plant. Her hair which cascaded down her back was a reddish bronze colour, very much like the colour of rusted cannons, he thought. Oh yes! the exact tinge of an old rusted iron canon! Pitambor remembered the huge iron cannon that was found when they were digging a well. It was said that the Burmese soldiers had left it behind when they had to retreat. He remembered that a group of students had come after some time and hauled it away.

After looking at her for a while, Pitambor plucked up the courage to speak to her. "You will get sick if you walk about in this foul weather, in this dirty muddy road," he said. She turned and looked at him, her face and eyes expressing a surprised curiosity. But like before, she did not utter a word in reply. "If you had only asked me I would have sent my servant to get you all..." But before he could complete his sentence, she turned to look back at him again. Pitambor felt as if her eyes that were burning with a fiery look would burn him to ashes! Without wasting any more time there he walked rapidly away and sat down on his usual seat on the stump of the teak tree. He glanced towards his house and saw that his wife had taken to her bed again. She had tried to get up that morning after a long time. Her wasted limbs creaked with a ghastly sound when she tried to lift herself up, and she felt dizzy, so she had to go back to her bed again. Now she lay there staring at her husband's comings and goings. Pitambor gazed at her with a cruel, and at the same time, somewhat embarrassed look. It was time for him to go and give her one of her medicines, and he was quite aware of it. But he did not get up — he simply sat where he was looking down contemplating his shoes. There were only four people in their *satra* who wore shoes — the clerk of the *satra* office, the two sons of the *'adhikaar'*, and he himself. He bent down and tried to clean his mud caked shoes with his handkerchief, and then looked up again at the road to see if Krishnakanta had come. But there was still no sign of him. As he sat waiting impatiently, a bullock cart came creaking into his compound. It was his tenant farmers bringing his share of the paddy they farmed. On any other day Pitambor would have rushed in enthusiastically and counted the baskets of paddy. But today, seeing that his master was absentminded and indifferent, the servant came and counted the baskets and stored them inside the granary himself. After some time, having rested and had some refreshments, the tenant farmers came as usual and took their leave from Pitambor. Also as usual, they had some complaints about Pitambor's tightfisted attitude. But nothing moved him today— he sat where he was, silent and indifferent.

Looking inside he saw that his wife was lying with her eyes open. He noticed that someone had replaced a tumbler of water near her, and he remembered that the time for her medicine was past. He got up and was about to go and give the medicine when he heard Krishnakanta's voice. Forgetting about his wife's medicine he quickly put on his shoes once again and hurried to the gate where the priest was waiting for him.

His wife's eyes, he noticed, seemed to be unusually weak, — the fire that normally gleamed in her eyes whenever she looked towards him seemed to be slowly dying out.

"*Mahajan,*" the priest called out.

"Yes Bapu. Tell me have you any news?" asked Pitambor.

"You will have to go to meet her on the coming full moon night in the '*dhekal*', the room containing the '*dheki*' (the wooden pedal for cleaning and pounding rice) behind her house." The priest looked furtively all around, and continued, "I have found out that she is not pregnant at the moment. Her daughter told me this after I had bribed her with sweets. It seems that it is not yet a month since she destroyed her last pregnancy. The girl is too young to understand these things. It seems that she had helped her mother by holding an oil lamp while the woman finished her job. She also told me that this time her mother had used a spade belonging to a Brahmin boy from Chataraguri. This boy used to come cycling from his home to study in the college near here. He is a boy from a well to do family, but loose of character. He came, and instead of going to college, he hid his books inside a basket of rice in Damayanti's hut and spent his time with her. He used to spend the money for his college fees buying things for Damayanti. This foetus she buried this time was this Brahmin boy's."

"Listen *Mahajan*," the priest continued, "I have spoken to her about you. At first she was quite angry! 'That Sudra man,'she said. 'How dare he even think about such a thing! Does he not know that I am the daughter of a good Brahmin priest?' I replied that everyone knew that she was a Brahmin woman. But now that she had taken the sinful path, there could be no difference between castes. I also told her that no Brahmin would stoop to marry her now. They would simply exploit her body and then cast her aside like the useless husks of the sugarcane stalks. I told her that you would marry her with all due rituals, as soon as your ailing wife died; that your wife was even now as good as dead. After you married her, she would live a good and prosperous life. Do you know, *mahajan*, when she heard all this she went into her hut and cried her heart out, I do not understand why. She came out after some time wiping her tears away and said, 'I do not keep well these days, and it would be a relief if I could lean on someone's shoulders.' I replied that it was not surprising that she did not feel well, after having aborted no less than five or six times within a short time; that if her case happened to come up in a Panchayat meeting no one would even consider going near her because anyone found to be giving her even a tumbler of water would be fined a sum of twenty rupees!"

"What other option did I have?" she wept. "My daughters were starving. The Adhikaar's wife used to ask me to do small jobs for her in the kitchen. But now she says that I am not fit to work in her kitchen, that whatever I touch will become impure and contaminated. Before I used to be asked to spin and make the sacred threads, the *'laguns'*. But now the Brahmin families of this area will not allow me to make the *'laguns'*. They say that I am corrupted. The tenant farmers know that I am all alone with no one to look after me or my interests. So they too have started behaving like monsters. What do they care that I am a lonely Brahmin widow with two small daughters? How can I fight them? I own some acres of farm land in Satpakhila, but I have not been given my share of five *maunds* of paddy ever since my husband died. I have not been able to pay the revenue tax for that land for three years, and the land could be auctioned off any day now. What was I to do? I had to think of feeding my two daughters."

But in the meantime Pitambor was getting more and more impatient. He almost yelled, "Yes, yes, I understand all that. But what about me— my case?"

"Yes, I am coming to that," replied the sly priest. "She said, 'He is a sudra belonging to the fourth caste. Having relations with him…' But finally she told me that she would meet you on the full moon night in the *dhekal* behind her house."

Pitambor could hardly contain his joy. And taking advantage of that Krishnakanta said, "But you will have to give me one hundred rupees. Damayanti says that she needs a mosquito net, and the two girls will have to be given sweets from Bhola's shop."

Pitambor hurried inside and went towards the small wooden chest he kept in a corner of the room. His wife opened her sick eyes and followed his every move. Suddenly he shouted at her, "What are you staring at? One day I will come and pluck your eyes out!"

Krishnakanta sat outside listening and understood what was happening inside the bedroom. He was a sly fox! When Pitambor came out and handed him the one hundred rupees he whispered, "If necessary give your wife a small pill of opium that night. She lies on that bed listening to everything, and understanding everything. It is better to be careful." And laughing meaningfully, the sly Brahmin priest took his leave. The woman on the bed simply shut her eyes.

Krishnakanta walked back a few steps and said, "Damayanti is very keen on money. She acts like a tigress where money is concerned. Never mind, you will be able to hold her hands intimately."

The *Mahajan* felt rather guilty, and looked back at his wife. But no, she had heard nothing. She was asleep. But her dried up forehead glistened with perspiration!

It was the full moon night of the month of *Aa'har,* (June/
July). Pitambor wore an *endi kutua* and a fine *santipuri dhoti.*
Across his shoulders he had thrown a *chador* of fine cotton. After
a long time today he brought out the mirror with the wooden
frame and scrutinized his face. He had shaved that morning,
and now out in the sunlight he could see fine wrinkles covering
his face, and he was somewhat disturbed. It seemed to him that
the wrinkles were a net and he was the fish trapped in the net
of his wrinkles!

At the appointed time he walked towards Damayanti's house.
It was located near the bridge on the Singra river, beyond the
forest of teak trees. Very few people of *satra* lived here, and it
occurred to Pitambor that Damayanti was able to live as she did
only because she lived in an almost deserted area.

He looked up to see some mushroom coloured clouds
floating in the sky, looking for all the world like some cannons!
And that round moon! As though it was a deer shorn of its
skin! — As though someone had come and wrapped the dotted
skin around the cannons! A skinned deer— its meat shaking
uncontrollably without the skin to bind it in place! Lovely
fresh healthy meat!! This skinned deer suddenly transformed
into Damayanti! A completely nude Damayanti! There were
her lovely breasts, like a pregnant goat's stomach. Her body was
the colour of tender bamboo stalks, and her lips? They were
soft and lovely like freshly cut mangoes oozing sweet nectar!
Pitambor could not stand there any longer looking up at the
sky, weaving fantasies about the woman! The place was deathly
quiet and completely deserted. It was the night of the annual

*Bhaona* performance and the entire village had gone to see it. Indeed she had purposely chosen this night!

He heard some jackals howling from the thorny shrubs nearby, and he walked rapidly to Damayanti's hut. He took off his shoes and sat on the plinth. A heady fragrance of the Champa flower floated out from somewhere. Damayanti sat with her younger daughter on a small cot set between the basket for rice and a dome of ripe jackfruit. The girl was drowsily writing the letters of the alphabet on a slate with a dirty old lamp with a broken chimney as the only source of light. Leaning against the wall, Damayanti was watching the man. After a while she beckoned to him to come inside and sit on a *'morha'* that was placed nearby. A small earthen lamp filled to the brim with mustard oil burned nearby. For some reason Pitambor was afraid to look at her body in the pale light of the lamp. He had a peculiar feeling that everything might be over if he did. .....  It was all a land of illusion, he felt. Was this Brahmin widow in front of him a real woman?

"Have you brought any money with you?" Pitambor was startled into reality! He had not expected her first question to be so very materialistic.

"Whatever I have is yours," he replied and handed her a cotton bag. She took the small bag and put it inside a cane basket that was hanging on one of the posts of her *'dheki ghar'*. In the meantime, the girl who was writing the alphabets went and lay down with her sister and instantly fell asleep. There was a very low cot in one of the rooms that was used to store the baskets of rice. Damayanyi's husband, who had been a priest, had been given that during the *shraddha* of the *'adhikaar's* brother.

Pitambor followed Damayanti and sat down on that cot. After a while, she came to him. ....

Two months passed by. One day, after the *Mahajan* had left her, Krishnakanta happened to see Damayanti bathing in the river, and made fun of her. "Why Damayanti, I never saw you coming to the river to bathe after you spent the nights with the Brahmin boys of Dudhnoi Bongora!"

Damayanti did not reply. But the sly priest was not put off. "I suppose it is because this one is of the Sudra caste....?"

Again she did not reply, but she suddenly jumped up and going to a corner she began to vomit violently.

For some moments the priest stood where he was dumbfounded. Then he said, "This must be Pitambor *Mahajan's* child then?"

Again she was silent. But Krishnakanta continued, "That is very good news. Poor Pitambor will be very happy. He was almost going mad at not having any children! I will go and give him the good news." After a pause he said, "Listen, you must not worry or feel bad. Our Gandhi Maharaj did not believe in all this business of caste. He said that all men were equal and the same. Just you wait and see. Pitambor will marry you with all the proper rituals as soon as his wife is dead. I am sure that you are aware that the villagers were getting fed up of your way of life and were thinking of having a Panchayat meeting about it. I don't think you know that some time back one of the things you aborted and buried beneath the clump of bamboo was dragged out by a jackal and deposited in one of the priest's courtyards.

And have you any idea how much that poor man had to spend to get himself purified — and for no fault of his own!"

Damayanti started vomiting again.

"Be careful, Damayanti," warned Krishnakanta. "Do not do anything this time. Even after knowing all about you and your repeated abortions, Pitambor is willing to accept you. If you do anything this time to damage the child within you, I tell you, you will go straight to hell. No one and nothing will save you."

And Krishnakanta went to give the *Mahajan* the best news he had ever heard! "Pitambor, if she does not go and abort this child, you can be sure that she will not be unwilling to marry you."

As usual, Pitambor was sitting on the stump of his favourite tree. He had not even bothered to take off his mud caked shoes. Hearing the priest's words he started trembling in sheer excitement. He would be a father! Could it be true? Would he really be a father at long last? But of course it must be true. The Brahmin priest himself had told him so.

He stood up deeply agitated and started walking about aimlessly.

Krishnakanta said, "What is the matter with you? Why are you walking up and down like a monkey? But of course you have more than enough reason to be happy and excited! It is not a small matter to become a father after thirty years of waiting! A very great fortune indeed!"

Suddenly Pitambor came and knelt down in front of the other man. "Bapu," he pleaded, "please see that she does nothing to frustrate the dearest desire of my life. You well know what kind of men my father and grandfather were. Only a sufferer can understand the despair of a childless man! Besides, she is a Brahmin woman from a priest's family— and now she holds my life in her hands! What will I do, Bapu, what will I do?"

Krishnakanta lifted one hand as if in blessing and said, "I will keep track of her and what she does, like a vulture keeping track of a corpse. Do not worry. I will also warn the old woman who helps in these bad things. But I will need some money to bribe her too."

This time Pitambor did not have to go to his small box to get the money. That morning he had sold all the fruits from his seven Jackfruit trees, and the proceeds were still in his pocket. He took out the entire bundle of notes and handed it to the priest. Extremely pleased at the way his plans were going, Krishnakanta put his hands on Pitambor's head and blessed him.

Now when Pitambor went to the bedroom, his eyes fell straight on his sick wife's eyes. And in spite of himself, their sad and desolate expression moved him to compassion. But the next moment he regained his composure and he forced himself to anger. "Hey, you sick and barren woman! How dare you stare at me like that!" And he yelled out to his servants, "Come, come! Lift this bed. Take it to the small room next to the *'dheki'* room. Come, hurry up!"

No sooner said than done! Together with four of his servants Pitambor carried the bed together with his wife still lying on it, and put it inside a small, dark room without any sort of ventilation, near the room where the paddy and the *dheki* were placed.

Since his affair with Damayanti, Pitambor seemed to have

almost forgotten that his wife needed at least some looking after, and had to be given medicines regularly. She was just skin and bones now, and seeing that their master did not bother about her the servants too had started to neglect her. They were even careless about bringing her food on time, and often did not bother to bring her even a glass of water with her meals let alone give her the required medicines on time. The poor woman's throat would often become parched and dry with thirst, but she would not utter a word of protest. People said that she looked more like a corpse than a living woman. Even now, when her husband brought her to this small dark room and left her there she kept quiet. But surprisingly, even in the dank darkness her eyes shone brightly, and it seemed as though she saw and understood everything that was going on more clearly than if she was out in the open.

The very thought of fathering a child made Pitambor delirious with joy! He lived in a world of joyful imaginings. The child in Damayanti's womb seemed to him to be already a boy, then a young man. In Pitambor's imagination, the boy walked along the banks of the Dhansri river holding his father's hands! The ever joyous and sparkling golden thread that binds fathers to sons seemed to stretch happily far into the distant horizon, where all was sheer happiness, where the ties and traditions of family were an unbroken joy.

Pitambor got a couple of his trusted servants to bring down an old wooden box from its perch near the roof of his room. When he was sure that he was alone, he opened the box and took out a bundle tied in an old '*gamocha*'. In the bundle were a few pieces of half burnt bones, the *'ashthi'* of his long dead father, and entwined in the dried up bones was a chain of the precious *'poal'* beads that were so much a part of the traditions of Assam. Pitambor remembered how, as his father lay on his death bed, almost choking with the effort to speak, he had said, "Keep this chain of my *'poal'* beads carefully. Your son will wear it, and then his son, and then his son's son, and so on. It will be the living symbol, the everlasting flag of our clan..." The old man died before he could complete the sentence. Pitambor took out this chain now, then wrapped the pieces of *'ashthi'* in the *gamocha* again, and put the bundle back in the old box. Finally he called in his servants and had the box put back in its old place on the shelf.

Days passed into weeks, and weeks into months, and Pitambor became more and more impatient to hear some news. He had heard that a foetus that was five months gone could not be aborted, and he calculated that it was now three months since she must have conceived. As he waited, each day without any news seemed to become more and more unbearable. Each passing day loomed in front of him like a mountain he had to cross in order to gain access to his happiness and survive.

Almost every moment he seemed to hear the Brahmin woman's footsteps approaching him, and he imagined that she was whispering to him, "*Mahajan*, hurry up and prepare for the wedding rituals. I can no longer hide my condition. Do you not see how big my stomach is growing? Hurry up. Get the wedding preparations ready." Again, "All those things about Brahmins and Sudras, about Hindus and Muslims are just a lot of nonsense.

We are all human beings, and you will find that the same red blood flows inside all of us. ... Get the wedding rituals ready".

She seemed to walk with *ghungroos* tied to her feet and she came to him with tinkling feet! He imagined her lovely fair and slim legs. *"Mahajan,"* she seemed to whisper, "nowadays I do not bother to go and bathe in the river after I sleep with you. Go, get ready for our wedding."

Three months passed by uneventfully, and the *Mahajan* still dreamed of walking along the Dhansri river banks with his hands on the shoulders of a handsome youth— his son!

It was the month of Bhadra, (July/August), and often violent storms lashed the villages. A storm had been steadily gaining momentum since that afternoon. Going inside to shut the door of his wife's room, he noticed that her eyes today burned more brightly, more malevolently than usual. They looked to him like a shining snake that passed by him in the dead of night! As the storm raged, the lamps were blown out, and all other sounds were drowned out by its sheer ferocity. Pitambor shouted for his servants but no one could hear him. The only sounds to be heard were the rumblings and thundering of the storm, and of trees being felled, either struck down by lightning, or blown down by the fierce winds.

There, another tree had crashed down! Which tree was it? Pitambor wondered. Somewhere in the distance, he saw a streak of lightening that had definitely struck another tree! He could hear the frightening sounds of the tree being split down the middle and crashing to the ground. He went outside to see what tree had fallen — what disaster this terrifying storm had caused?

In a corner of the grounds, the fruits of seven of his coconut trees had been heaped up waiting to be sold. Now he saw his servants running about trying to salvage them and store them inside the *dheki ghar*. Some of the fruit still on the trees thudded on to the ground blown down by the wind. No one could hear anyone... But gradually the storm began to abate; the rumblings and thunder died down, but heavy rain lashed the village. Lighting the lantern again, Pitambor could now see the heavy raindrops, and he could still hear the tinkling sounds of Damayanti's '*payal*' shod feet coming towards him!

Suddenly, amidst the rain, Pitambor heard someone calling him by his name. Picking up the lantern he hurried outside and saw the priest coming towards him completely drenched and shivering. Pitambor was frightened! Only some extreme news could have prompted the man to come out in this terrible weather! Krishnakanta held an umbrella over his head, but it had so many holes that it afforded no protection whatsoever. His *dhoti* had been drawn up to his knees, and only a thin *chador* that was dripping wet covered his bare body.

Holding up the lantern Pitambor shouted out, "Bapu! What brings you out in this foul weather, so late in the night?"

Somehow Krishnakanta managed to come and sit down on the plinth of the house. Leaning the torn umbrella against a post, he took off his *chador*, tried to wring it dry and wiped his wet face with it. Then pointing a shaking finger at Pitambor he said in a choking voice, "Pitambor, when your first wife died there were three inauspicious stars in the ascendant— three '*puhkars*'. Three or four?"

"I do not remember," replied the *Mahajan*. "Why?"

"When three *'puhkars'* are found at the time of the death of a person in the house, even the *dubori* grass shrivels up, and dies. When your first wife died, there were three puhkars. And as a result, even now the ill effects are there. Everything is dead and gone!"

"What has happened, Bapu? What is wrong?"

"She has spoilt it, *Mahajan*, she has aborted! She refused to carry the seed of a Sudra man! She belongs to the highest Brahmin clan, a woman from the Sandilya *gotra*! She has spoilt your seed Pitambor; she has finished her pregnancy!"

(The youth holding Pitambor's hands let go and fell into the deep Dhansri river! Who fell? Was it Pitambor, or the young man? Dear God, who was it that tumbled and fell headlong into the deep waters of the river?)

One day, soon after this, Damayanti heard a sound near her house in the dead of the night. Someone was digging something beneath the clump of bamboos behind her *'Dhekal'*. She shouted, "Who is it? Who is there?" and awoke her elder daughter. The six year old girl and her mother stood near the window listening. The sounds of digging came from the same place where the two of them had gone in the dead of night two days ago and buried that thing the woman had ruined. Mother and daughter had gone out that night and dug the hole with the spade the Brahmin boy from Chataraguri had given them. The young girl had quivered in fright when she heard the jackals howling nearby! And today the unmistakeable sound of digging the earth came from that very same place! Thud, thud! Thump,

thump! Standing near the window the two of them saw a lantern burning at the spot, and in the light of the lantern they saw the figure of a man, a strong, well- built man digging away at the very spot where Damayanti had dug just two days back! Indeed, he was digging up the same hole!

Damayanti's entire body and soul trembled at the sight! The man was Pitambor *Mahajan*. He had hung his lantern on a branch of the bamboo, and was digging religiously at the spot! The man had assumed a terrifying aspect, and he was hacking at the earth like a mad man! She trembled in fear and terror! Should she shout? Yes, of course she must. Such a terrible thing was happening in her own house— of course she must shout!

"*Mahajan*! *Mahajan*!" she shouted. But there was absolutely no response.He simply kept on digging.

"*Mahajan* why are you digging up my ground?"

Pitambor looked up towards the window but did not utter a word.

Damayanti went almost wild with agitation. "Yes, I buried it. But what will you find there now? It was just an unformed lump of flesh."

Pitambor lifted his head and looked at her. "It was my child! I will at least feel the flesh of my flesh! I will feel my child, my son and heir, with my two hands!"

# IN SEARCH OF MARTYRS

Six years ago, in 1999, I found myself in a cemetery where the relatives of some of the dead buried there were moving around in a confused manner trying to locate the graves of their loved ones. They were from Taiwan, and I was told that they had been conscientiously searching throughout Dibrugarh and its neighbouring areas for whatever they could find about their lost relatives.

I had heard many stories about the last Great War from my mother and some other relatives from our village of Amranga in South Kamrup. We used to go to Amranga quite frequently when we were young children, and there we spent our time playing with the village children on the sands on the banks of the Jagalia river. Sometimes we used to ride on the elephants also, and I used to cry out in agony when I saw the scars on their foreheads, made by the sharp equipment the mahouts used to guide the elephants. The wounds were so deep that the raw flesh became exposed, and I could not tolerate the thought of the agony of the animals. Trainer elephants ('*Kunki*' elephants) were used at a small place called 'Rani', to train the newly caught ones. My brother, Mantu, and I were taken there to see how the training was done. I am told that I screamed out, "Don't bring me here, please don't bring me here again!" when I saw the cruel way in which this "*kheda*" was carried out. I remember that the animals under training wept in pain and agony all the time they were being trained, and tears poured down their cheeks continuously. I could not have been more than four or five years old at that time. I remember that the roads were so bad that our old Ford car had to be dragged along by the elephants.

My brother Satyabrata and I sometimes rode on our elephant to the banks of the Jagalia River. Kilt, the mahout, would take the elephant into the deeper part of the river and spend hours bathing it there. And I remember that when they came out of the water the animal's back was full of tiny black 'elephant leeches'. All the children used to help to pull out these leeches from the elephant's back! These scenes are still very vivid in my memory. I had heard people saying that a contractor of the village had made a lot of money during the war by selling these leeches to some of the soldiers camping in this area. There were many such reminiscences of the Great War among the older generation of the area. We used to play among the ruins of the many barracks that were still discernible. I remember an odd saucepan that one of the old grandmothers had used for boiling water— she told us that a black soldier had given it to her.

But to come to our beloved elephant... It seems that our family had a number of elephants at one time. But only one remained by the time we were old enough to visit our village. But one day, this very dear animal, on whose back we spent almost all our time in the village, went '*musht*'— got loose somehow and trampled a number of villagers to death. He became so violent that the people of Mirza were scared to go out even during the daytime. In the end, the Government was compelled to order the elephant to be shot to death. This incident too is still vivid in my mind and even now tears fill my eyes when I think about it.

A few days ago, I read Tarquin Hall's book entitled, "*To the Elephant Graveyard*", which the highly reputed newspaper, "*The Daily Mail*", had praised saying that it was "A wonderful book that should become a classic." It was published by the famous publisher John Murray who lived in Albemarle Street in London. One of the book's main attractions for me was that it gave detailed descriptions of the experiences of the well -known elephant expert of Assam, Sri Dinesh Choudhury. In fact, Tarquin Hall had dedicated the book to Dinesh Choudhury. I had known Sri Choudhury since my childhood, and my elder brother Satyabrata was a great friend of his. I am mentioning this because this book has a chapter on how elephants that had gone wild *(musht)* could be cured. After I had read this, I thought with regret that maybe our elephant, the dear playmate of our childhood, would not have had to be killed if a man like Dinesh Choudhary had been around at the time. I was very intrigued to read, and to hear from him, how he had even saved some elephants that had been ordered to be killed. I thought that Sri Choudhury could be compared with Jim Corbett, because Corbett had a similar deep understanding of the character and the ways of tigers. Jim

Corbett too I knew, gave deep thought to the actual condition of a tiger before agreeing to allow it to be killed. The people of Garhwal called him the *sannyasi sahib*. I feel that everyone should read this wonderful book by Tarquin.

As I have mentioned, we used to run around the ruins of the army barracks near the Jagalia river and spend our time playing all sorts of games there. We also heard many stories about the soldiers who used to go wherever they wished and whenever they wished, around the villages of the neighbourhood. The young maidens were so scared of them that they used to hide from them in the deep bamboo baskets used for storing rice. It seems that there was some bombing somewhere around the area too. Our aunts told us that the bombs burst like so many crackers, and that a peculiar flame, like huge fireworks, erupted from them. The maidens hiding in the rice baskets were given the signal that the soldiers had gone, and that it was safe for them to come out, by the ringing of bells. An aged elephant trapper had the responsibility of sounding the signals. I was told that once the old man forgot to ring the bell in time, and as a result, one of the maidens had been raped by a soldier who had sneaked in from the back compound.

I had also read many fearful stories about the Japanese soldiers who had come as far as Kohima. In the jungles of Kanchanaburi I had met the families of some of the soldiers who had survived the war. I saw some beautiful paperback books in their homes. I have not seen any Assamese books with such attractive covers, except maybe for a book by the writer Bikash Barua, about his travels to foreign countries with his family. This was probably the only Assamese book that could boast of a beautiful and attractive cover.

The people of our '*satra*' could not tell me with any certainty how the Negro and other soldiers had come to Jagalia. Sometimes, the young daughters of the 'Gosain' family would hide among the tall bamboo, and other trees with thick foliage, and sneak glances at the white bodies of the soldiers when they came to bathe, naked, in the river. I had also heard a lot about one Gilmil *sahib*, who had come to the neighbourhood when he was appointed as manager of the Bordoa tea estate situated near our '*satra*'. He had married a girl from the Rabha tribe, one of the tribes of lower Assam. One of his sons had been killed in the war. Gilmil *Sahib*, it appeared, had been granted the right to hear criminal cases. There was one particular story about him which was very popular among the villagers. Once, when he had gone out hunting, he had shot a wild pig. At exactly the same moment another bullet had hit the animal. The second shot had been fired by Purna Choudhury and curiously enough, both bullets had lodged at exactly the same spot in the pig's stomach! Gilmil *Sahib* came and stood by the dead animal. Almost immediately, Purna Choudhury appeared at the spot with his double rifle on his shoulder and claimed that he had shot the wild pig. Gilmil *sahib*, in the accepted '*shikar*' dress of khaki half pants and felt hat, yelled, "No! I fired the shot that killed it." The people who had gathered around could only watch in surprised curiosity while the two hunters shouted and argued. As both bullets had lodged in exactly the same spot, no one could judge whose bullet had actually killed the pig! It was a very curious case indeed!

A terrible argument ensued between the *Sahib* and Purna Choudhury, who was a wealthy and arrogant man. Unable to tolerate the vile language of the equally arrogant *sahib*, Choudhury lost all sense of balance, and came near him and gave him a mighty kick in the bottom! In great anger, the white *sahib* strode to his elephant that was tied at the Mirza road crossing, and went straight to the magistrate of Kamrup district. But, the story goes that the *'hakim'* (magistrate), said, "*Sahib*, you are the one who hears and judges all the criminal cases here. So why don't you judge this case yourself too. But remember one thing, if you consider a duel, you will be allowed to shoot just one bullet at Sri Choudhury!"

The villagers of Barihaat trapped the *Sahib* in a very intelligent way. They said to him, "*Sahib*, Choudhury always comes to the *'haat'* (the weekly bazaar), in Barihaat in a white horse drawn buggy. It will be easy for you to shoot him with just one shot as he crosses over to the bazaar."

Gilmil *sahib* aimed and shot at the turbaned figure, clad in a white outfit with a *'chador'* around his neck, just as the buggy was crossing over, and the horse drawing the buggy disappeared from view. But it was not Purna Choudhury on the buggy; it was only his image! When the *Sahib* came to know the truth he did not get angry — instead, he laughed heartily!

There were also many tales about the soldiers who had stayed back after the war. I had also read many stories about Manabu Wada of the 3rd Battalion, 138th Infantry Regiment, and other soldiers who had invaded Kohima, in the book, *"Tales by Japanese Soldiers"*, edited by the Japanese soldier, Kazuo Tamayama, and John Nunnely.

These stories, written by the Japanese soldiers themselves, were very curious and also heart-rending. Reading these, I was reminded of the cruel manner in which the conquering forces treated the Japanese while building the infamous bridge on the river Kwai. Most of these Japanese soldiers had hardly crossed their boyhood. Manabu Wada's father had come to drop him at the place, and the boy had tied his few belongings in his *'Furioshiki'*, (a piece of cloth tied around the waist), and handed them to his father. As they were climbing the harsh, craggy 3000 metre high mountain, the peaks had become covered by a thick fog. Wada had written, "Our horses and the donkeys carrying our baggage and our food supplies fell into the deep gorges so we had no food. I saw dead bodies of the enemy strewn all over the place. These dead bodies had become infected with gangrene and looked horrifying."

He had written many different accounts of the terrible times he had gone through; for example, "The 138th Regiment has no rations. The British have burnt down all our depots." Or,

"We were being bombarded with heavy and medium artillery, but we had just a handful of shells..."

(I had heard some hair- raising tales of the Imperial Japanese Army which had invaded Imphal and Kohima. Some 305,000 Japanese soldiers had fought in the Burma war between the years 1942 and 1945, and 180,000 of them had died.)

One of the most heart-rending stories had been written by Yusumasa Nishiji, a soldier of the 20th Independent Engineering Regiment.

("It was the last phase of the Pacific War of 1944. There

was a fierce battle between the British and the allied Japanese forces, and the latter had received orders to retreat across the Burma border. There are no words to describe the frightful and harrowing conditions the retreating soldiers had to face while crossing the Yu river. Everything was in a state of utter chaos and confusion. There were hordes of half dead soldiers lying around, waiting for their release through death. No one knew, or bothered about what regiment one belonged to. We called this road, the 'Human Remains Road'."

On one page, he narrates the tale of one particularly indomitable soldier. This soldier had displayed extraordinary courage and bravery on the battlefields of Hong-Kong and Singapore. He was lying half dead on the road, his once healthy body reduced to a mere skeleton. Drenched by the heavy monsoon rains he was trying to crawl across the Chindwin river. But just before he could reach the banks of the river he died. Wada had written, "I saw that brave figure dying there, right in front of my eyes, and I could do nothing to help him.

There was hardy any chance of the wounded soldiers proceeding any further. The badly injured ones were given a grenade each… two men would hold each other tightly with the grenade between them, and the grenade blasted, the small remains of their bodies would be flung far across the area."

I also could not forget the stories of the inhuman torture inflicted by the Japanese upon the British, Indian and Australian soldiers who had invaded Kanchanaburi. But I can find no adequate language to describe the harrowing and heart-rending conditions of the Japanese soldiers who retreated from Kohima and Imphal in March, 1944.

It was the year 2000. The Indian Oil Corporation (IOC), Assam Oil Division, had invited me as Chief Guest at their celebration of the 550th birthday anniversary of Sri Sri Sankardev.

I had been to Digboi several times before, and every time, the authorities there had made very comfortable arrangements for my stay. But this time, I was put up at their luxurious new Guest House located amidst the most beautiful natural scenery. Someone had pointed out to me, "See, those are the Patkai mountains. Su-Ka-Fa entered Assam through those peaks."

Su-Ka-Fa was the Ahom King who had installed the Ahom rule in Assam six hundred years ago. So many accounts and stories came to my mind...

He had brought some scholarly historians with him, and they had written that the huge elephant that he had ridden on, was buried alive in the dead King's tomb. I wonder if this horrifying story was true!

The area surrounding the Guest House was beautiful, with varying hues of green, with lovely trees and wild plants all around. Suddenly, some of the window panes of the lovely house shattered into bits. When I asked one of the officers there what had happened, he replied very casually, "A herd of wild elephants came and broke them. They also overturned several vehicles that were parked near the Guest House.." I was also told that this was quite a common occurrence — that herds of wild elephants came this way quite frequently. Everyone is familiar with the story of elephants and the smell of oil. Elephants have a peculiar liking for the salty taste of mud mixed with oil. As we all know, the British were quick to learn this fact and to take advantage of it. But the elephants have no idea that this important oil town of today was founded through them.

I had heard that the Japanese soldiers had utilized elephants when they invaded Imphal and Kohima, as these animals can maneuver the most difficult of terrains.

Someone told me that he had heard on the BBC news that an old cemetery dating back to the 2nd World War, had been recently discovered in Assam, and that on hearing this news, the relatives of many young soldiers killed in the war had come to Dibrugarh seeking this cemetery. Sixty three years had gone by, and the relatives still had no idea about what had happened to their loved ones. So, they had now come with great hope and anticipation to distant Assam, seeking information.

After the meeting celebrating the 550th Birth Anniversary of Sri Sri Sankardev was over, I requested one of the Administrative officers, Prabin Bora, "I have heard that the newly discovered war cemetery is not far from here. I would love to see it. Can you help me?"

He very kindly arranged a car for me with a driver named Prem Kumar Gurung. He also sent a photographer and an armed security guard with me. A young officer, Sanjib Rajkumar, accompanied me. Rajkumar was a writer, and he was as handsome as a real prince.

We started early next morning, heading towards Joyrampur. Although it was only September, there was a heavy fog. The road was narrow, and it was bordered on both sides by thick forests.

I had heard that some of the forests of Africa were so thick that even birds could not fly through them, and now I thought birds would not be able fly through this jungle either.

Sanjib Rajkumar said, "We will have to travel along the famous Stilwell road for some distance." Stilwell, as the Commander of the British troops had built this road using local labourers at the cost of great suffering on their part. It was a story that could well be compared to the story of the sufferings of the soldiers of Kancnanburi.

The Member of Parliament, Dr. Arun Sarma, had once told me that he wanted to revive this abandoned Stilwell Road. It would link Ledo in Assam with Mang-yu in Myanmar, and it would also open the road between the Post World War-1 Burma road to Kunming in China.

We arrived at the Dihing Tea Estate after driving for almost fifty minutes. I had heard the sounds of wild elephants a number of times as we drove along the thick jungles, and I thought to myself, 'What will happen if these herds of wild elephants suddenly came out and attacked us! Our armed guard would be quite useless.'

The driver, Gurung, pointed his finger and said, "Can you see that bridge over the Dihing river over there? The British built it, and they treated the labourers with almost inhuman cruelty in the process."

Rajkumar said, "There were some British owned coal mines nearby, and the overseers treated the miners very badly. Conditions were so bad, and the treatment was so inhuman, that many of the labourers and miners ran away, unable to withstand the torture and the sickness— the dreaded *Kalazar* that was rampant there. But they were always captured as they tried to cross the bridge over the Dihing and were forced to work again."

As we proceeded, I saw some wound-like scars on the sides of the hills. I was told that they were the result of the cutting down of trees and the frequent blasting that went on there.

We crossed Lekhapani and Miwau, and entered the National Highway No 38 This was the starting point of the famous Stilwell road.

We saw a cinema hall almost in ruins. The word "Stilwell" was written in faded letters. Very soon, the thick, almost impenetrable jungle started again, and sounds of elephants breaking bamboos could be heard off and on. I am sure these forests were very helpful to the Allied army when they drove away the Japanese soldiers. Who knew when a herd of wild elephants would appear from the deep jungles and trample our car to bits! I felt that the wild beasts were hiding somewhere very near us! I am sure the hapless soldiers often had to face such herds as they were fleeing.

Joyrampur was situated on the border of Arunachal Pradesh. Our car stopped at the check post there and our papers were thoroughly scrutinized. The natural scenery all around was so breathtakingly beautiful that my soul seemed to become one with it. After driving for a short while, we saw the camps of the Assam Rifles scattered all over the area.

After a short distance, we arrived at the newly discovered cemetery, and I noticed a signboard as soon as I alighted from the car. The signboard read as follows: "2nd World war Memorial Cemetery. These graves stand as a memorial of the combined efforts of thousands of unlisted soldiers, workers and administrators, whose ingenuity, efficiency, dedication, and never say die attitude in rigours of blistering heat, jungle malaria, and monotony ultimately accomplished the great task of fight against Fascism. A saga of great determination." But there were no epitaphs on any of these graves — no sign of any personal touch — as there were on the graves in the War Cemetery at Digboi .Many were the people who came crowding to this place hoping to find some sign of their loved ones. But they had to return disappointed. There was nothing, absolutely nothing, to identify anyone. On one of the graves at the War Cemetery of Digboi were the words, "T J Evans, a Corporal from Lancashire, who died in December, 1944. He gave the greatest gift of all — his unfinished life."

On the grave of the young RE Carr, were inscribed the words: "While you sleep in peaceful sleep, your memory we shall keep."

I wonder whether anyone had thought of those poignant words of that great poet, Jalaluddin Rumi:-

"When you leave me in the grave
Don't say goodbye.
Remember a grave is only a curtain
For the paradise behind."

No, there was nothing at all on those almost ruined graves. These were graves covered with untidy wild climbers and dirty green moss. Graves that had been trampled upon by herds of wild elephants and broken to bits. There was a deep, unbroken and heartbreaking silence reigning over the cemetery.

We entered the graveyard. There were hundreds of graves,

all of them in ruins. We could hear the sounds of the elephants making their way through the dense jungle. Some bricks from the broken graves lay scattered here and there. The letters "B&Q: 119" were inscribed on these bricks.

I stood silently for a while near some of these graves that were now protected property. There was one that was Major Hsia Chu Ching's. He was the Company Commander of the 2nd Battalion of the 10th Regiment and Independent Engineers of the Chinese army stationed in India. It was written on his grave that he was born in the year 1913, at Wevi in the Heple Province, and that he died in the year 1943. I had heard that about 2000 Taiwanese soldiers had been buried here.

Later, I read an article in the Assamese journal, *'Prantik'*, written by Sri Surendranath Barua. It was entitled, "The graveyards of the 2nd World War Joyrampur" (*Dwitiya Mahasamarar Ekhan Samadhi Khsetra, Joyrampur*) *Prantik*, 16th March,2004, page 47.I had read there that in the Hong Kong valley, across the border of Burma and India, altogether eight battalions of the Chinese army were used to curb the Japanese, from the capital city of Kachin Province right across to Burma. Three battalions had been sent ahead before the others. Their main camp had been installed at Lekhapani, and they also had a transit camp, and a dispensary at Margherita. The dead soldiers were buried in a graveyard situated three miles away from Lekhapani.

I went with Rajkumar to meet the person who had discovered the cemetery — Col KSRathore. Rathore was a strapping and energetic young man. His shirt front was covered with medals

— symbols of military gallantry and bravery. I asked him how he had managed to discover the cemetery after so many years.

He replied, "You might say that I discovered it almost by accident. While on patrol I happened to see a truck loaded with old bricks. I captured the truck and asked the driver where those bricks had come from. He guided us to this graveyard. We saw some broken graves. There are still many such graves inside the forest. It was only with great difficulty that we could clear the jungle and reach the graves."

Rathore told us a strange thing: "We had doubts about the genuineness of these abandoned graves. Were they really graves of dead soldiers? Then one day, I saw something like a white stick poking out from a cracked grave. After examining it, we found that it was not a stick, but the bone of a leg of some unfortunate soldier. Now, we were sure that this was indeed a cemetery dating back to more than sixty years. When the media released the news of this discovery, crowds of relatives of the soldiers started coming here. Most were from Taiwan. They used to light lamps and pray here. So, we held an official ceremony in memory of the dead. That was in the month of February, in 1999.

Now every Saturday and Sunday we come to this cemetery, play bugles and pray for the souls of the dead buried here."

I went forward to some graves lying in the deeper part of the jungle. I thought I saw a herd of wild elephants rush through the forest at great speed. It seemed as though a cluster of dark clouds had blown across my field of vision. The armed security man came and reminded me that it was time to go back.

I saw some bushy trees blossoming with fiery red flowers, and

I remembered how, when we were children, we had gone hunting for such flowers, the "*bahaka*" flowers, in our village, Amranga. I also remembered a certain General of the Eastern Command, who had one day presented me with a bouquet of red roses.

This General had once recruited a very poor Muslim boy dwelling on the footpaths of Delhi to the army at my request. I will never forget his kindness.

I thought that since he was in the Eastern Command, he must have known these areas very thoroughly. But he was not able to discover this cemetery. Now, I thought that the red roses given to me by the handsome man, as handsome as the actor Charlton Heston, or Burt Lancaster of the old movies — were very similar to the red flowers blossoming beneath the teak trees of this area near Lekhapani.

Suddenly we saw a herd of wild elephants preparing to come down towards the road, and we beat a hasty retreat.

What is the past? Is it not, too, a grave? — a grave covered by a piece of fine, soft, silk material? Love too is but one of the traps of death...

So many thoughts came to my mind...

We returned. A deep and heavy sadness filled my mind. Yes, we returned in utter silence.

# ISHWAREE

Ishwaree Devi had heard about the preparations the members of the Ramayan group of Sri Dham were making to attend the International Conference at Janakpuri. She had hoped for a letter regarding this from Dharma Bahadur Rana, one of the members of the group. She had met this young man at the Ramayan Mela at Chitrakut, and she knew that he had lost his wife in a dreadful motor accident. Many people, she had heard, had perished in that same accident. However, no letter had arrived from Dharma Bahadur.

Ishwaree Devi was a widow. She had felt a strange attraction for Dharma Bahadur from the first day, and in time, she had come to believe that one day she would become his wife, and thus be able to start her life anew. This was one of the main reasons that she had hoped for an invitation to attend the Ramayan Mela at Janakpuri this year. She was aware that Dharma Bahadur also hailed from Uttar Pradesh.

The invitation letter came — from Sri Mahananda Shastri,

the father figure of Sri Dham's Ramayan group. She was both
pleasantly surprised and touched at getting a letter from him.
His assistant had written the letter and Shastriji had signed it.
He had written with great affection,

*"This time the Ramayan Conference has been organized at Janakpuri,
the birth place of Janaknandini Sita. I have observed that you attend
this conference every year with great sincerity. I have also read all
the articles you have written on the subject and I have been greatly
impressed by the depth of your knowledge and the range of your
research. But, as you have seen, we have to give time and scope to
the foreign delegates and guests to read their articles and speeches.
Besides we also have to allow time to the scholars from different parts
of our country too. You have seen how some of these Ramayan lovers
and scholars get so engrossed in their own deliberations that they get
carried away and do not want to stop! You must have noticed too
how we have to carefully divide the time among the guest lecturers,
taking care that none of them feel offended or ignored. But this time,
I will try my best to fit you in. So bring a good article with you. You
will definitely get a chance to read it at this conference. We plan to
meet at the New Delhi railway station on the 28th of November, and
catch the Magadh Express to Patna. We should arrive in Patna at
seven thirty in the evening. The Sri Ram Mandir of Patna and the
'Nagarpalika' will be organizing a meeting that evening. The foreign
delegates will also be introduced to us at this meeting. This time you
will not be left out. From Patna, we will catch the bus to Raxaul,
where the passports of the foreign delegates will be checked. And after
we have cleared the immigration formalities, we will proceed straight*

*to Birganj, from where it is only a four hour journey to Janakpuri. It is winter, so you will be able to see the snows of the Himalayas! Bring sufficient warm clothes with you. May Sri Ram Chandra bless you. Your well wisher,*

*Shastri (Gurukul Dham).*

Sashtriji had never written such a long and detailed letter to her before. She had received only impersonal printed invitation letters to the last three Ramayan conferences that were held at Chitrakut, Ayodhya and Ujjain. And this time she had received this long and affectionate invitation! She was deeply touched.

Ishwaree folded the letter and put it carefully in the envelope. She realized that Sri Mahananda Shastri had read the articles she had submitted for the last three conferences only now. And maybe he had even felt some kind of guilt at not having been able to fit her into the programmes the past three years.

But guilt? Why should such a great man feel any guilt for such a minor thing?

Ishwaree was filled with a sense of humble gratitude...

She tucked the precious letter into her blouse so that she could read it again later on.

Like a bright streak of lightening, she remembered Dharma Bahadur Rana, who had accompanied the Ramayan *'Mondoli'* to Chitrakut, Ayodhya and Ujjain. She wondered whether he would be with them this year too. Would he too be paid his air travel expenses, like the scholars who were doing their research work in countries like Russia, Thailand, Belgium, New York, London, Malaysia, and Java? Shastri Maharaj liked him a lot. And not without reason, she thought. The presentation he had made on the Adi Ramayan had been excellent and of great significance in the field of Ramayan research. She had been astounded by the comparative study he had made of the Indonesian 'Kakabin' Ramayan, Java's 'Ram Keling', 'Sheriram', the 'Ramkiyen', and the 'Ram Jagan' of Burma. Some people said that Dharma Bahadur Rana had got many rare manuscripts concerning the original translation of Goswami Tulsidas's Ramayan, from the archives of the Scottish Church College of Calcutta. He had also discovered some very valuable manuscripts of the translation of the Ramcharitmanas that Mr.Grouse had left behind at Mathura.

Ishwaree was not sure whether Dharma Bahadur was indeed a devotee of Sri Ram. It was rumoured that at the conference at Ayodhya he had said that he would become a devotee of Sri Ramchandra only when he could prove that Sri Ram was really a historical figure. There are so many versions and myths regarding Ram— the story of the priest in '*Taittiriya Aranyak*', who prayed for a 'Ram' ,that is, a son like Sri Ram, by abstaining from meat, and from his wife, by not drinking water from any vessel etc., but the same Ram is manifest as Rama, a prostitute, in the '*Taittiriya Samhita*'. Then, there is the Brahman Ram of '*Oitreya Brahman*', Nripati Ram of the '*Rigveda*', the philosophical Ram of the '*Jaimaniya Upanishad*'. It was not easy to dig out the actual historical Ram from all these versions. Indeed, it seemed almost impossible. Yet Dharma Bahadur Rana was unrelenting in his efforts to find the one true Ram from amongst all these legends or myths— whatever these may be.

Ishwaree was convinced that Dharma Bahadur was already

a devotee of Sri Ram, even if in some deep recess of his heart. Otherwise, where would he have found the strength and the perseverance to continue his difficult and painstaking research for so long?

She could not think of him as merely an impassive scholar. She had felt a strong attraction for him ever since the first time she had met him, and she was certain that emotional sensitivity and scholasticism found equal place in his heart. She had come across numerous scholars when she had accompanied Shastriji's group to places like Ayodhya, Chitrakut, Ujjain etc., and she had always thought that the arrogance of some of these intellectuals was scandalous. She would never forget how she had been put to shame when she had tried to talk with one of these men at Ayodhya! She had gradually reached a stage when she found scholars of this type almost loathsome. Indeed she thought that there was very little difference between these snobbish *'pundits'* and the ruthless butchers! — Intellectuals who had no universal human love in their hearts were as good as corpses inside their coffins, she thought. A person might be a great scholar— But that did not necessarily mean that he was a truly *good* man. This seemed impossible, but it was nevertheless true. Such scholars seemed to find an almost demonic pleasure in exposing the ignorance of others. Ishwaree had herself been a victim of such behaviour and she had seen ample proof of it in the conferences she had been privileged to attend. But she did not believe— could not believe that Dharma Bahadur Rana could be like that.

Ishwaree felt Shastriji's letter pressing against her breast, and she became extremely eager to accompany his group. She longed to meet Dharma Bahadur once again.

There was nothing to stop her from joining the group, because she was, in a way, totally alone in this wide world.

Her mother had hailed from a place called Ukiyam situated on the southern bank of the Brahmaputra, and her father had been a poor priest from Uttar Pradesh. He had met Ishwaree's mother when he had gone to Ukiyam once on his priestly duties. She herself had been born in Munshiganj.

Finally, unable to bear their terrible poverty any longer, her father had left his priest's work and moved to Bhadoi to work in the carpet factory there. All her brothers and sisters worked in the factory too. But since she had always done well in her studies, her father had allowed her to pursue her studies. All the children had read the *"Ramcharitmanas"* at home, and Ishwaree had also known how to sing the verses in tune. In time, she passed all the Rashtrabhasha examinations, and went to join as a teacher in one of the schools for Harijan children in Delhi. She had to send almost her entire meagre salary to her ageing father who lived in a barrack of the carpet factory in Bhadoi. The school authorities gave her accommodation in a tiny *'barsati'* near the school.

Ishwaree studied the Ramayan with great devotion and sincerity, and whenever possible, she made it a point to attend any discussions and seminars on the Ramayan. In due course, she had married a teacher working in the same organization as her school. But he had lost his life in the 1984 riots in Delhi when he had rushed inside a burning house to save the life of a Sikh child. Ishwaree felt a sense of shame and guilt at the attraction she felt for Dharma Bahaur, after the death of her husband.

She arrived at platform number six at the New Delhi Railway station at seven o'clock in the evening, in order to catch the Magadh Express. She was wearing an old and worn out overcoat. She could not afford to buy a new one. She carried papers, pencils, pens, etc., in a *khadi* bag slung over her shoulder. She had written a long article on Sita which she hoped to present at the International conference. She had taken a lot of pains over and she was sure that since Shastriji had written personally to her inviting her to the conference and telling her to write an article, she would definitely get a chance to read it. As a precaution she had made two copies of the writing. She had one copy in her bag, and had packed the second one with her clothes in the canvas suitcase.

The Magadh Express steamed into the station as she began to search for Shastriji's group on the crowded platform. It became almost impossible to move in the frenzy of the passengers scrambling for the train! She managed to board the train, and started looking in compartment after compartment for her travelling companions. She saw no one from the *'mondoli'* in the first class compartments and as she passed along the second class compartments, she spotted the saffron clothes of Shastriji. She had no idea when the members of the Ramayan group had entered the train. As she sat clutching her *khadi* bag and canvas suitcase, pushed about by the frenzied crowds, Ishwaree felt like a restless caged bird. She did not know whether Dharma Bahadur would come to the conference or not and she was aware it was this uncertainty that made her so restless. All the others seemed to have come. She caught a glimpse of the Russian scholar, Veskovitch, and the internationally famous Belgian intellectual, Herbert Hondin. She also saw Mr. Dylan from Guinea, and the Ramayan devotee from Bangkok, Srisurang Pulthupi, and so many other well-known faces. Ishwaree was well acquainted with the golden mop of hair of Herbert Hondin, the tall and angular figure of Dylan, with his prominent cheek bones and thick spectacle frames. Elizabeth O'Hara, the British lady who lived in an ashram in Brindavan was also there. Her rather long, pointed nose and her bright blue eyes could be seen clearly in spite of the saffron sari she wore, covering her head in the fashion of the *sannyasins* of Brindavan. There was another *sannyasi* trying to keep his balance among the crowds, holding on to the bunk with one hand and his walking stick with the ther. The passengers near him had to lean sideways in order to avoid his matted locks of hair. He found it difficult to hold on to the old worn out blanket he had wrapped around himself! Suddenly Ishwaree almost lost her balance as someone pushed violently against her in the mad rush of passengers struggling to find a seat.

It was only when they had almost reached Aligarh that Shastriji was able to organize the seats of all the members of his Ramayan group. Together with his *munshi*, Rajtilak, he went around the train, asking after the welfare of all the persons who had come as members of the group of Ramayan lovers under his supervision. It was not easy to meet every member among the pushing crowds of humanity that overfilled the train. But

Shastriji was an experienced traveller. He had travelled along many an almost impassable path in the Himalayas, had walked the hot, burning sands of deserts many times. So it was probably not much of a problem to find and look after the comfort of the people who had undertaken this journey with him.

Ishwaree found that her heart started pounding with anticipation as the *munshi* and Shastriji approached her seat. She was not sure whether this was because Shastriji had personally invited her to attend such a prestigious international conference, or whether it was because now she would be able to find out whether Dharma Bahadur had come. She had found a good window seat, and near her was a rural family from the east Champaran district. A group of young boys were sitting cramped into the seats opposite. Their conversation made it clear that they were Bihari students of Patna University.

Shastri Maharaj saw her, and came forward eagerly. *Munshiji* took out his list of "*mondoli*" members travelling in the same group, and marked her present. Ignoring the crowds, Ishwaree bent down and touched Shastriji's feet. He said, "Ishwaree , I knew that you were a devotee of Sri Ramchandra the very first time I met you. May Sri Ramchandra bless you..." Before he finished speaking, the *munshi* bent forward and whispered something to Shastriji. He spoke to her, "Ishwaree , *munshi* is right. Three Sri Ram devotees have come from Belgium and France with just one week's notice. They are our guests. If necessary, I will ask you to vacate your seat for them. *Munshi* will arrange a seat for you in the Ladies' compartment."

She nodded but was a bit apprehensive. She remembered

how, on her way to the Ayodhya Ramayan Mela, she had had to travel for almost ten hours sitting hunched up on a tin trunk. That time too she had had to vacate her seat for a foreign guest. But then, pushing all such thoughts to the background, she almost shouted out, "Maharaj, Maharaj! Has Dharma Bahadur Rana come? I did not see him."

Shastriji stopped short in the midst of the pushing crowds. He said, "Yes, he has come. He and a party from South India left for Patna by the morning train. But we will all be together during our journey from Raxaul."

The angular and rather rough looking *munshi* almost dragged the Shastri away. There was no time to stand and talk. There was a lot of work to be done. All the members, foreign and local, had to be organized. The passports had to be scrutinized, and so on and so forth...

A golden door seemed to open up before Ishwaree's eyes! Dharma Bahadur Rana had come! No, no! What was she thinking? She was filled with a sense of shame and guilt. Here she was on the way to the holy birthplace of Sita— the manifestation of the goddess Lakshmi Devi— but where was her mind? What stirred her eagerness?

Just a few days back, she had read a verse written by a Persian poet struck with sadness at the sorrow of Sita. It had so impressed her that she had written it down in her notebook. She had met the student, the Sri Ram devotee, Kuttubuddin Mocha, at the Ramayan festival at Chitrakut. She started quietly reciting some lines about Sita written by the famous Persian poet Firdausi. Indeed, it was only after Sita's death that her greatness and courage was realized and understood!

*"Uske morne parhonth who baat
Kah nahi sakte.
Uski bataana tab hota hai jab
Who jhul jati hai.
Kahne ko stri hai, lekin barhe
Barhe bahaduron se barhkar hain."*

She must have been reciting these words to herself in a low voice because the Bihari woman sitting next to her happily breast feeding her baby, uncaring of the passengers said, "If you want to sing, sing loudly, so that we can also hear the song.

Ishwaree smiled at her. To whom could she reveal the reason for her eager joy! The train picked up speed. One thought, one emotion, filled her entire being, like a reptile wrapping itself around her body. The water bottles, the various suitcases and bags of all sizes and shapes, the tiffin cases, the holdalls, the people surrounding her, young and old— even in the midst of all the chaos and the crowds, that one thought alone filled her mind and pushed aside everything else. The waving green paddy fields in the distance with the mud huts around them; the vast expanses of yellow mustard fields looking as though someone had spread a large yellow handkerchief over the ground. The newly harvested *bajra* fields— all that she could see was, as it were, enveloped and surrounded by that one thought and emotion. In some places, the ends of the harvested *bajra* crops had been tied up ready to be carted away. These she thought looked from a distance like corpses tied up in mats ready to be carried away for cremation. And those kindling charcoals— like the burning sparks of a cremation fire? Probably these fires were intended to fertilize the soil before the next sowing?

A peculiar and strange thought filled her mind. She seemed to find a strange beauty in everything around her, and this she thought, was due to the unusual sensation in her mind. Dharma Bahadur Rana and these fields— the sheer beauty of nature seemed to intoxicate her, and she felt that the elements of nature and the man had taken on the shape of a necklace around her neck— the man and nature being the bright jewels in the necklace! The man, the elements of nature and her mind became one inseparable unit. Hundreds of melodies and sweet songs crowded her mind, and she sang a verse from Iqbal out loud so that the woman breast feeding her baby could hear her, a verse extolling the greatness of Sri Ram.

She saw the flames in the fields but felt no change in her mind today. Until just a few days back, the sight of a fire would set her screaming in fear, and tearing her hair! The doctors said that this was because of the shock of seeing her husband burnt to death. But today, that fear seemed to have disappeared.

Ishwaree seemed to come out of a trance.

She saw the priest of the famous Chaturbhuj Sriram Mandir, Pandit Krishnapada Sewak Swami coming towards her. He held his bundle of clothes clutched to his chest with his right hand and was holding his walking stick in his left hand.

Shastriji's *munshi* was probably so busy with the foreign guests that he had no time to think of his countrymen, no matter how scholarly or respected they might be! Ishwaree had never had a high opinion of the *munshi*. He was always more interested in people with money than in real scholars, and he took more pains with these persons.

Seeing the elderly Pandit Krishnapada, Ishwaree jumped to her feet and took the bag from his hand. She then pushed her way through the crowds and somehow managed to bring the old man to her seat. She wondered for a moment why he had taken such trouble at his age. But then she realized that this conference, where so many devotees of Sri Ram gathered from around the world, was like a call to the soul— a call from Sri Ram and Janaki Devi! Anyone, young or old, could follow this call.

She went forward, then stood still surrounded by the crowds at a loss to understand what she should do. The narrow aisle was full of passengers, going to, and coming back from the toilets. There were so many people that they bumped against each other as they came and went. After a little while the woman with the baby somehow managed to make some room near her for Ishwaree, and she thankfully squeezed herself into that tiny space. As she sat down, she saw Gajapati Mishra, the highly reputed Ramayan scholar from Vrindavan coming towards them. He was looking displeased and was muttering under his breath. He was probably unhappy this time also with the arrangements made by Shastriji's Ramayan group. He had been delving into the various aspects of the Ramayan for the last twenty years and his knowledge was encyclopedic. That is why, probably, he came eagerly to each conference, with a large bundle of manuscripts. Everyone was aware of the erudition of this man, but Ishwaree had noticed that he had never been given the chance to present his articles in any of the three conferences she had attended. She

*Remnants of colonialism / while worshipping culture*

remembered that a couple of Western beauties, with their short bobbed hair, their high heeled shoes, and painted lips, had been given time to go on the platform with a Belgian scholar and sing verses from Tulsidas! But Gajapati Mishra, who had spent almost his entire life researching the Ramayan was not given a chance to make his presentations! This time too, it appeared, he hoped to be able to share his monumental knowledge and learning with other learned delegates at this great conference. Ishwaree sprang up and offered her seat to him. The entire area was filled with the smell of very old manuscripts written on barks of trees, and of old blankets. The woman with the baby who now covered her nose with a piece of cloth was not happy. Now Ishwaree had no seat. She pushed past the crowds of passengers and tried to go forward. A group of armed security men were sitting near the door. They looked meaningfully at her and started passing lewd remarks. So she returned to her former place near Gajapati Mishra's seat and somehow managed to sit down on his iron trunk.

Ishwaree had no difficulty in getting down from the train at Patna station. She only had a *khadi* shoulder bag and a small canvas suitcase. But Gajapati Mishra was not so lucky. He had his walking stick and the bundle of manuscripts, as well as his bedding and trunk. He found it difficult to disembark from the crowded train, loaded as he was with all these things, and it was only when Ishwaree went forward and relieved him of his large bundle of manuscripts that Mishraji was able to get down.

The station master, and some members of the Patna 'Ramayan *Mondoli*,' were waiting at the platform ready to receive

*Ishwaree is too eager to please the scholars. She gives up her seat everytime*

them in the traditional manner, with marigold garlands. The members of the Ramayan *Mondoli* looked healthy and well-fed. They were all dressed in spotless white *Khadi*, with the typical *'uttariyas'*, or *chaddars*, slung over their shoulders. Their foreheads were marked with streaks of sandalwood. The station master, on the contrary, looked thin and underfed. His trousers and black coat hung loosely on his emaciated body. As soon as Shastriji and the scholars with him alighted from the train, the devotees of Sri Ram from Patna came forward and garlanded them with marigold garlands and sprayed fragrant *'attar'* on them. Ishwaree too looked very much like a devotee with her long flowing hair and the garland around her neck.

A *'shamiana'* (a wall-less *pandal*), was put up next to the platform, and a meeting was held to felicitate the Ram *Mondoli* members. In the meantime, the delegates from Russia had arrived by air. They were the great scholars Dr Sakharov, and Pamela Ludmilla. As soon as they entered the *pandal*, they were nearly smothered as their admirers garlanded them. Their clothes were almost drenched with *'attar'*.

Ishwaree glimpsed Dharma Bahadur Rana among the crowds in the *pandal*.

She had hoped that he would come and sit next to her on the bus to Raxaul. But she saw that he had given all the comfortable seats to the others of the party and had chosen a seat at the very back with Shastri Maharaj's *munshi*. It was a thirteen hours' journey from Patna to Raxaul, and she wondered whether he would be able to travel so far in that uncomfortable position. She noticed that he looked thinner than when she had last seen him at Ayodhya .He had also grown a beard. The beard, she thought, emphasized his attractive masculinity even more than before. Even the spectacles with the thick frames perched on his elegantly pointed nose, seemed to lend an unusual brightness to his face. Ishwaree longed to sit beside him, and try to find out— by tactful, indirect questions— whether he still missed his dead wife, whether his grief for her had lessened somewhat. Now that he had started to move around with the Ramayan *Mondoli*, involving himself in their various works, he must surely have reconciled himself, at least to some extent, to his loss. She longed to sit near him and talk to him and tell him so many things. Tell him, for example, that she no longer fainted away at the very sight of fire. Her doctors said that this was a natural effect of the passage of time. But she knew that Dharma Bahadur was also responsible for it to a great extent.

Christina, a young British lady who had been living in Barsana Baba's temple near Vrindavan for almost eight years, sat next to her on the bus. She was a tall and slim lady with golden hair. Her beautiful blue eyes made her very attractive. She was dressed in a sari worn in the *Vraj* manner, with one end covering her head. She had already won the hearts of all present with her recital of extracts from the *Ramcharitmanas*, and the *Padabalis*. But Ishwaree was somewhat cynical— had she really forsaken her country and family and friends because of her devotion to Sri Ram alone? Or was there some other unrevealed reason?

Shastriji's deep and sonorous voice could be heard above the din: "Our foreign guests should have their passports and other documents ready. They will have to clear immigration formalities at Raxaul."

Christina fished for her passport in her shoulder bag and as she searched she muttered, "What is the need of passports etc? All humans are, or should be, free beings from the moment of their birth. I want to become an Indian national, and yet..."

After having lunch at Manihari, the passengers boarded the bus and took their seats once again.

They started travelling through the beautiful countryside of East Champaran district, along the golden mustard fields that seemed to stretch to the horizon, and the open, and fallow *'Bajra'* fields that had taken on the colours of camel skin.

Ishwaree did not get a chance to talk with Dharma Bahadur at Manihari either. The women in the group all sat on one side, while the men sat on the other side. So she too had no other option than to sit with the women and have her lunch. As they sat together on the bus, Christina pulled her sari end tighter over her head and whispered to Ishwaree, "I don't like sitting next to men. You know why, don't you? Most of them are always after the pleasures of the flesh."

In the meantime it had started to get dark, and the western sky became tinged with a reddish hue. Gradually the sky became darker with the colour of pieces of ancient ruins. Then the world became completely hidden behind the dark veil of night.

Seven hours passed by, and they arrived at a place called Sitamari. Suddenly there was an uproar among the passengers. "Foreigners are not allowed entry at this ckeck post. There has been a mistake; we took the wrong road!"

Shastriji's sonorous voice was heard, "What has happened? Have we left the Raxaul road?"

The driver got annoyed. He told them sharply that he had come this way because he had the permission to take both foreigners and non-foreigners alike along this check post.

The bus started moving again. The road was clearly illuminated in the bright light of the vehicle's strong headlights.

It arrived at the security gates at the border and stopped near a wooden bridge. A group of armed security guards surrounded the bus, while some others started to scrutinize the Ram *Mondoli* banner that festooned the front of the vehicle.

Shastriji, together with his *munshi* and some of the important members of the *Mondoli*, crossed the wooden bridge and walked quickly towards the small immigration office. The bright lights of the bus illuminated a portion of the bridge which seemed to lie there like the remains of some huge dead animal. It was this wooden bridge that drew the lines of the border between two countries.

But why boundary lines? thought Ishwaree There could not be any boundaries in the world of men. These lines of control, and borders between country and country were nothing but the signs of man's cruelty. Human beings had no right to draw any borders and lines of differences among themselves. All were God's children.

Christina slept soundly through all this.

Dharma Bahadur Rana was one of the persons who got down at the check point. But soon they hurried back, and Shastriji's *munshi* shouted to the driver , "Not a single one of the foreign devotees with us will be allowed to enter here. Even their passports are not sufficient to allow them entry at this point. You have again taken the wrong road."

All the people on the bus were greatly perturbed. Even those who had been sleeping soundly woke up in the tumult.

*Munshiji* spoke again, "All Indian nationals will be allowed to enter, but no foreigners. What do we do now?"

Shastriji spoke up, "If necessary, we will go all the way back to Raxaul. It will be very unfair to even think of deserting our foreign guests in this forest and go on to Janakpuri."

All the passengers hurriedly boarded the bus again,.

This incident and the others— seeing the sannyasins who lived in the inspection bungalow at Sitamari, at midnight; seeing them in the early dawn, bathing in the river and chanting the Gayatri *sloka*; and then arriving next afternoon at Raxaul, filled with soldiers of the Border Security Force— all these passed across Ishwaree's eyes like a dream.

Long lines of trucks were parked along the road to Raxaul, and near the immigration point, waiting for permits to cross the border. The foreign delegates were asked to keep their passports ready and get down from the bus. Shastriji reminded them that if they had anything to declare they should go immediately to the Customs and Immigration counter and show whatever they had. All the foreign guests took out their cameras, tape recorders etc — all the things they thought should be declared.

Ishwaree also got down with Christina and went to a nearby dhaba for a cup of tea. There was a big hoarding in front of the dhaba, and Ishwaree translated for Christina's benefit, "Anyone entering Hindustan from Nepal from this point should carefully read all that is written in this notice."

They read the notice together. It said, "It is forbidden to bring any foreign goods to India. Stainless steel utensils etc. made in Nepal will be seized at this point, in accordance with the Customs regulations."

They wandered around the Immigration office for some time. But all the while, Ishwaree's mind was with Dharma Bahadur. There seemed to be some problems with the immigration papers of the delegates from China and Belgium, and he was busy with them. And this blue- eyed Christina who was with her— her eyes seemed to flit to the foreigners again and again!

The entryway to the kingdom of Nepal here was truly a magnificent sight! The massive ivory coloured gate was adorned with beautiful paintings of golden stars and flowers; of elephants, lotus flowers and the Goddess Lakshmi Devi. His Holiness Sri Sankaracharyya had inaugurated this gateway many years ago.

The immigration formalities did not take long. *Munshiji* collected the passports from the foreign guests and preceded them to the immigration office. When they came back they were all wearing marigold garlands!

It was past midnight by the time they arrived at Birganj.

They found that everything had been arranged for them. The guest house of the Rani Sati temple was run by the 'Seva Trust', so their accommodation had been arranged there. This temple had been built on the ground where a Sati had been murdered!.

No, No! It was sacrilege even to think of such a thing! This was the most hallowed ground of a *mahasati,* of a most pure and holy woman! Inside the temple, there was a marble statue of the Sati, sitting with her dead husband's head on her lap. The statue shone with the bright red vermilion smeared all over it and the green *'bel patta'* (the leaves of the wood apple tree, beloved of Siva).

The delegates had all rushed towards the beds made up comfortably on the floor of the guest house. But Ishwaree stood bowing low in front of the statue. There was one question bothering her— was this a sacred piece of land, or was it an evil ground where a murder had been committed? She felt a strange hesitation to look up at the face of the statue and she stood vacantly in the vast marble courtyard of the temple.

Gradually, the sounds of the weary travellers quietened. Everyone had already taken the most comfortable beds.

Ishwaree had no idea how long she had been standing there when suddenly her trance was broken by a voice calling out to her, "Ishwaree, Ishwaree! Why are you standing here like this?"

Startled, she looked back and saw Dharma Bahadur Rana standing not two feet away from her.

She could not say a word in reply...

Dharma Bahadur, however, did not have the time to linger there. He went forward to meet a devotee who was coming out from the Ramchandra *Mandir*. She had met this devotee in Chitrakut and Ayodhya. He would sit in wet clothes after bathing, and repeat a particular Ram *mantra* one thousand times, from midnight onwards. He had spread a deer skin he had carried under his arm in readiness for his *'japa'*. He had matted hair and was dressed in saffron clothes. But he removed his saffron *chaddar* and bared his emaciated body. Even in this extreme cold, he sat bare bodied on his deer skin and started his meditation.

The conference *pandal* in the Mozalia camp was vast. Ishwaree sat in one corner with some other delegates. The conference had started, and Shastriji had already introduced the important guests and delegates who were sitting with him on the platform He started with the guests from abroad, whom he introduced with great pride, and then he introduced the members of the *Mondoli*. He had introduced Ishwaree too, at the conferences at Chitrakut and Ayodhya. But this time, at holy Janakpuri, he seemed to forget all about her! In the meantime, many scholars had arrived from Kathmandu. Ishwaree doubted that she would get a chance to read her carefully prepared article that day. Her knowledge seemed very insignificant compared to the profound learning of the highly respected *pundits* who had congregated at the conference. However, she consoled herself thinking that she was unusually fortunate to be able to listen to the scholarly deliberations of some of the top Ramayan scholars of the world.

On the second day too, the erudite scholars started the session with deliberations and discussions on various scholarly topics regarding the Ramayan.

A group of established scholars, of the likes of the elderly intellectual, Acharyya Khemrah Keshav Sharma, went on the platform in order to deliberate on the topic "Role of the Ramayan on the formation of the Hindu Kingdoms."

There were heated debates on various related subjects. There were discussions on the duties of Kings towards their subjects, and vice versa, citing examples from the ancient texts, like the *Rigveda*, the *Yajurveda*, etc. These great learned scholars spoke about the power of the meetings and committees mentioned in the *Atharveda*. The vast conference hall echoed with the *mantras* of the *"Krishna Yajurbaidik Aitiriya Sanghita"*. And sitting in her corner Ishwaree listened to the famous statement Sri Ramchandra had made at Chitrakut, "The only path of a King is the path of Truth and belief in God— religion. No religion can be greater than Truth, and a King takes the path of Truth for the sake of his subjects."

And then, there was that question Sri Ram had put to Bharat at Chitrakut, "Have you been able to sacrifice the fourteen faults for the sake of the welfare of the subjects?" Fourteen faults!!

And the famous declaration of Sri Ram Chandra, *"Janani janmabhumishya swargaadapi gariyashi"* — one's mother and motherland are greater and more glorious than the heavens themselves.

Then there were discussions on the devotees of Ram during the '*Licchabi*' age— and of the great devotion to Sri Ramchandra of the kings of the Sun dynasty, and the story of the historic Ram *Mandir* on the banks of the Bagmati river.

The topics under discussion ranged from the role of the Ramayan in the formation of the Hindu nation state based on religion and Truth, put forward by the Acharyya Khemraj, to myriad other such serious and significant subjects. Ishwaree sat and listened to the Acharyya's paper on this topic from her inconspicuous corner.

Suddenly Ishwaree felt dizzy. She seemed to be saying to herself, "Hindu kingdom, Muslim kingdom, Christian kingdom— what is the significance of all these? Are the people of a Muslim kingdom living in peace? Has not blood flowed like fountains in the middle of the Arab deserts? All those Christian countries of Europe are forever fighting against each other! So, where is the sense of talking about different kingdoms?" Then she felt somewhat ashamed at her thoughts.

The second half of the second day was given over to deliberations on the topic of "Youth power and the Ramayan". As the discussions started, Ishwaree heard a young man from Trinidad shouting that, "such conferences had become useless platforms for long-winded scholars; that they did not have the awareness and comprehension required to present the actualities of the modern youth's power and strength."

Another voice was heard, hard and sharp as an arrow. "Sri Ramchandra shot an arrow into Bali's back and killed him. We are not willing to accept the reasons and arguments scholars put forward to try to absolve Sri Ramchandra of this heinous act." "We also do not accept the arguments for Sri Ramchandra's slaying of Sambuk. It is clearly written in Valmiki Ramayan's *'Dakshinatya Sanskaran'* that Ramchandra killed Sambuk because he read the Vedas in spite of being a Sudra. We want to hear some just deliberations on this issue."

A number of the assembled scholars stood up and protested, "This student is not acquainted with the many unrelated incidents etc., that are part and parcel of the Ramayan. Valmiki did not write at all about Sambuks slaying or about Sita's entry into hell."

"That's right. Different sects and different countries have played havoc with the original Ramayan of Valmiki, pulling it this way and that, just as people fight over a piece of rare venison."

"There is no mention at all of the incident of the killing of Sambuk in either the 'Gauriya' edition or the 'Uttariya' edition of the west. Tell him to read the writings of the foreigner Butler Sahib— of Kamil Bulke Sahib! That young man, he is getting so heated up, it seems he will break the microphone itself now!"

"A King like Sri Ramchandra came down to earth!" said someone.

"Yes! Sri Ramchandra was one of the *'avatars'*, one of the manifestations of Lord Vishnu himself! A manifestation of *Parambrahma*!!"

"Once these people get on to the platform they don't want to yield place to anyone else!.. Don't they have any sense of time at all?" declared someone.

"There are so many other learned scholars waiting to present their papers."

"It seems as though they will come to blows now over this issue of Sambuk!" said another.

Ishwaree came out from the conference hall, confused and shaken. The article she had prepared and written with such care and hope was already quite crushed. She tried to console herself by thinking that at least she had been happy while writing it. This was enough, she tried to think. Suppose others did not hear it— so what? She had heard so many curious things today. That itself was enough for her! For example, she learned that the turban, that according to the Malaysian Ramayan, Sri Ram's mother had woven for him, adorned the royal head of the Muslim Malaysian King, Yang Dee Pertuan Angag!

She also learned of the faithful devotion of the royal dynasty of Thailand for Sri Ram. She also heard the painful and intriguing story of the banishment of Sita... The portrait Sita was supposed to have drawn of Ravana travelled to so many diverse places — to Kashmir, Sri Lanka, Indonesia and Java. This portrait changed form and face so many times!... But had Sita really painted a portrait of Ravana?

After coming out from the conference venue, Ishwaree searched all over for Dharma Bahadur. But the man seemed to have vanished.

The *sannyasis* who had come with their group had set up a separate place for themselves in some tents in front of the general camp, and they lived their daily lives there without bothering anyone else. On her way to the conference that morning, Ishwaree had seen one of these holy men sitting facing the sun, in a complicated yoga pose. Now, on her way back, she saw the man sitting at the same place in the same pose.

What kind of test was this, she thought, tormenting one's body in this manner! She had noticed that the Swamiji of Sri Ramchandra temple, had spent the entire journey from Birganj silently uttering *mantras* with his beads. He had not even drunk a drop of water on this long and arduous journey. Now, she saw that he was sitting near the tents, the colour of dried camel skin, reading a pile of papers. The papers were so old that they looked like the old manuscripts written on barks of trees. She thought that he must have been writing an article, taking a lot of trouble and care over it. But he did not get a chance to get on to the stage and present it. Was he upset about it? she wondered. He had spread some sheets of paper out in the sun; Did they get wet somehow? Ishwaree was not so disappointed at not getting a chance to read her article, but she was distressed that the old Swamiji was not given time to present his paper.

Arriving back at the guest house, she found that many of her fellow travellers had already returned. There was no end to her surprise. Dharma Bahadur Rana was among them, walking towards the Janaki Devi temple with some of the ladies of the group.

Seeing Ishwaree returning with her papers, two women clad in saffron commiserated with her, "You did not get a chance to make your presentation, did you? Never mind, do not let it sadden you. Three ladies from our group could not read their articles either. They had spent four years researching for their papers. Still, they were not given time to read them."

Ishwaree did not know what to say. Again the ladies spoke, "Dharma Bahadur Rana is taking us to various places of interest, like the Janaki Devi temple, Sri Ramchandra temple, the marriage hall etc. Why don't you come along too?"

Ishwaree had been astonished to see Dharma Bahadur outside the conference hall. She could not understand why he had come out before the end of the session. It was not usual for a recognized scholar of Sanskrit literature like him to leave midway through an important session.

There was a huge crowd of people from different parts of Nepal around the Janaki Devi *mandir*. The wedding of Ramchandra and Sita Devi had taken place during the dark half of the month, the *"Krishna paksha"*, and this was *krishna paksha*.

People had congregated here from places as distant as Dhankutar, Jajarkhat, Chamghas, Bharatpur, Chautara, Gorkha, Bidur, etc.

Ishwaree felt an intense sense of pleasure standing with Dharma Bahadur in the courtyard of this vast temple. All her troubles, all those big and small problems that beset her life seemed to vanish at this moment. At the same time she was overwhelmed with a feeling of shame at her feelings and emotions. She felt it was improper to have such feelings, standing in the beautiful temple the highly religious Maharani of Tikamgarh had built, spending all her wealth on it.

It was not too long ago that her husband had died, and here she was, already thinking of another man in this manner! It was shameful! Was she an unchaste woman then? Maybe, all immoral women were like her... — Sita reference ·

A group of devotees entered the temple with cymbals and drums in their hands, and Dharma Bahadur said to his group, "Go to the back door and enter the marriage hall from that side. Leave your shoes here, I will be waiting for you here. Leave your shoes here, I will look after them."

There were just two days to go before the anniversary of Ma Sita's wedding, so there was a huge crowd.

There were some rowdy young men sitting beneath the *shamiana* specially erected for the occasion, and there were some sitting at the ticket counter also. Seeing Ishwaree and the two other ladies with her, the boys shouted, "You have come from India, have you not? If our relations with India had been good, there would have been a far larger gathering of Indian pilgrims here today."

One of the ladies of the group asked, "You young men have also come to see the celebrations at Janaki Devi temple, have you not?"

"We are all unemployed youths," they answered.

"We had to pay the Govt thirty five thousand rupees to get this job of selling tickets at this marriage hall. And unless we pay them the remaining three lakhs, sixty five thousand rupees within the next fifteen days, we will land up in jail. Our job is to sell tickets and take photos."

"The Indian Government has opened only two of the fifteen doors," they continued. "Now the crowd of devotees has dwindled so much that only about ten per cent remains. Otherwise, we would have been able to make a very good profit at this Sri Ram-Janaki wedding festival."

"But why are healthy, young boys like you without jobs?" one of the ladies asked.

"We are men who have felt the sting of the whip," they said. "We sought freedom… we were imprisoned too. And now, our blood is the colour of black ink!"

All the young men smelt foul. One of them went very near Ishwaree and said, "If there is something you want to smuggle in just tell us. We have friends in all the police outposts. If there is something special you want… tell us. We have our people everywhere, and we are not afraid of anyone. We told you our blood is black, like ink."

The bells kept on ringing and pilgrims kept on pouring in…

Ishwaree, accompanied by the two other ladies from the *Mondoli*, walked rapidly towards the marriage hall. One of them, who was very religious spoke as she walked, "Valmiki has described how, at one time, this Janakpuri, fertilized by the rich silt of fifteen rivers was full of flowers and fruits. This Masthura has been known by so many names — Vaidehi, Tairamukti, Yagyakshetra, Kriyapith, Vaijanta, and so many more. Sita's dowry consisted of numerous cows, gold embroidered carpets, and horses and elephants. The accompanying soldiers were decked in jewellery studded with precious stones."

Another lady, shorter than the others, sighed and said, "Have you noticed the people who inhabit this Janakpuri now! They wear jackets made in China, and hats made in Russia. But their feet are bare! And they are thin and weak like starving people!"

"You are right," another woman said. "They have no petrol, no kerosene. Their businesses have almost closed down. Their relations with India are not good."

"I heard somewhere that they were collecting weapons from China," said another pilgrim.

"But one cannot eat weapons! Have you not heard that the Chinese are moving about freely around Raxaul? The other day a minister's brother was heard to say that if the smuggling business is stopped, this country will topple over like a house of cards."

Ishwaree was in no mood to hear all this. She went quickly to where Dharma Bahadur was keeping watch over their shoes. An unprecendent thought played in her mind — it was as though she had discovered a rare and precious treasure! That sense of shame and guilt that had weighed upon her mind for so long, like some old and hard rock was gradually decreasing! And all her conscious thoughts had come and assembled in one place!

Dharma Bahadur was still very close to her when they stepped on to the stone courtyard of the Sri Ramchandra temple. The crowds that had gathered at the Janaki *mandir* on this holy *Panchami* day of the bright half of the sacred month of *Aghon*(December/January),to witness the annual marriage festival, had spilled over to the Sri Ramchandra *mandir*, and there was a huge crowd in front of Ram Panchayatan, Lakshmi Narayan, and the Dashavatar statues there. It seemed that, from ancient times, the priests of this temple had been *sannyasis*. As Ishwaree and the two other ladies of the *'mondoli'* walked in, accompanied by Dharma Bahadur, they could hear the temple band playing a haunting melody — an ancient tune.

As she had walked along with Dharma Bahadur, holding a marigold garland in her hand, Ishwaree felt as though she were walking towards a wedding hall, that this Dharma Bahadur was her bridegroom and she was his bride!

The two women of the *mondoli* shouted to her, " Go on Ishwaree, go forward!"

Even when she stood in front of the priest, she was in her dream world! The loud voices of the two tall women jerked her back to reality.

"Maharaj Chandra Shamsher, it is said, had gilded the roof of this temple. And look at its condition now! See where they are throwing all the garbage!"

The other lady addressed the priest, "We have heard that the organization runs the temple. But all of the priests are bone thin as though there was a famine here!"

The priest who was getting ready to perform the '*Aarti*' (the evening worship) said, "The government pays us only twenty rupees."

Another woman said, "The boys at the wedding hall had shouted that their blood was nowadays as black as ink — that priests of many temples were compelled to take to stealing. Tch, tch! What a state to be in!"

The temple band was playing that same haunting tune as they did the ritualistic circumambulation of the temple. And Ishwaree was still following Dharma Bahadur like a shadow.

The precincts of the temple were filled with naked and semi-naked *sadhus*, and each sat in front of his own small fire. But unlike earlier, Ishwaree was not horrified by these many flames; she did not scream in fear and tear at her hair. Her grief for her husband who had burnt to death in the Delhi riots was still alive in some deep corner of her heart. But now, at this moment, the flames seemed to be like the sacred vermilion on Sita's forehead. They did not look like the bloody tongue of the blood drinking Chamunda Devi!

These *sannyasis* had come for Janaki's marriage festival on the fifth day of the bright half of the month. They had come from far away places — from Uttar Kashi, Tibet, and the Vindhiya mountains, and perhaps from the deep, isolated caves of the Himalayas.

The tunes the band was playing became more and more haunting; the smoke from the fires of the sannayasis blackened the dome of the temple, and their matted hair and the ancient ruins of the temple seemed to take on the same dark colour.

In the meantime, many of the pilgrims had lain down and

Hus highlights the fight for democracy in Nepal

fallen asleep wherever they could find some space. These weary people had travelled from distant places to participate in this great annual festival. Some had even lighted small fires within the temple precincts and were busy cooking their meals. Some were busy winding up their small stalls selling glass bangles and vermilion that had taken on the colour of old mud. A group of women were lying on the ground nursing their babies, their bare breasts hanging down like the nests of the golden 'tokora' bird.

Ishwaree felt as though she was coming out from some paradise together with Dharma Bahadur. She had never felt such a heavenly bliss in her whole life!

On the *Shukla Panchami* day, (the fifth day of the bright half of the month), some of the members of Shastriji's group opted out of going to the festival, and got ready to go to the banks of the Dhanusha and Kamala rivers. Another group decided to go past the limits of the city, across some of the most sacred spots like Bihar Kund, Purandarshar, and Madhyamshar, along the path the famous Mainu Baba was said to have cut out, and go and take a holy dip at Lakshmanshar. The 'brahmacharis' from Chitrakut and Ayodhya had got up before dawn and started their holy circumambulation, a path of two and a half 'krosh' (one *krosh* measured eight thousand hand lengths).

Ishwaree was totally immersed in her thoughts of Dharma Bahadur. She no longer felt any desire to even think about the main purpose of her journey — the Ramayan Conference and the article she had so painstakingly prepared for it.

Dharma Bahadur stayed very close to Ishwaree even when they stood beneath the huge banyan tree at Dhanushar. Legend has it that some bits of Sri Ramchandra's bow still lie scattered at this place. In fact, she and Dharma Bahadur bent over together to examine the pieces of the bow that were said to have become mingled with the roots of the tree. The bow was of a curious colour.

It looked as though pieces of rusted steel were lying scattered about. Ishwaree bent over and examined the curious pieces of the bow, touching them with her hands. It felt as though she was touching rusted steel. It was said that bronze was mixed with these roots. Here she was, actually touching the sacred and famous bow of Sri Ramchandra, but her mind was....

All her thoughts, all her feelings seemed to flow like a river and gather at one, and only one place! She wondered whether Dharma Bahadur's mind and emotions were in a similar state. In this holy place, was he too feeling as she was feeling?

He too was bending over and touching the pieces of Sri Ramchandra's famous '*Haradhanu*'. The tall and craggy *Brahmachari* from the banks of the Baitarini river was standing near him. Touching some pieces of the bow that looked like the trunk of an elephant he uttered a *mantra* under his breath.

The group from the '*mondoli*' arrived on the banks of the Kamala river, and getting down from the bus they set foot on the sands of the sacred river.

Even the crippled *brahmachari* from the temple near the Betrawati river, followed the others and stumbled forward as best as he could. He was a short and rather thin man. His cheek bones stood out prominently and his hair was matted. He carried a peculiar canvas bag. But he was very articulate. Speaking in a loud voice so that all could hear him, he said, "According to a legend, this Kamala river is actually the daughter of a Brahmin from the Mandarchal mountains. Through his devout meditation he had earned a boon from the goddess of the River Ganges. The belief was that anyone taking a holy dip in this river on the *'Makar Sankranti'* day would get his/her wishes fulfilled ."

But Ishwaree was in no mood to hear the *Brahmachari's* words.

The waters of the Kamala were not deep and one could almost see the uneven bed of the river. A few of the pilgrims became quite excited and waded into the river. She too slowly walked to the *ghat* facing the bridge and waded in.

The remains of a big fire could be seen on the bank. Someone had, it seemed, burnt a huge branch of a tree, and the charred remains looked like the burnt limbs of a big, black wild buffalo. And some half burnt pieces of firewood lay scattered on the river bed, looking very much like a golden coloured buffalo.

Ishwaree pushed at these half burnt pieces of wood with her feet. She tried to kick the pieces and throw them far into the river. But they would not move — the current of the river was too weak to drag them along.

Suddenly she heard a rough voice shouting at her. It was the *Brahmachari* from the banks of the Baitarini river. He shouted, "What do you think you are doing? Come away quickly; those are the remains of dead people!"

Shocked, she sprang back onto the bank with a strangled cry.

Dharma Bahadur was standing there with the *Brahmachari*, not knowing what to do or say. He had never been a very vocal person. But Ishwaree felt annoyed now. Surely he could have said something to comfort her or to make her feel better now.

On the way back to Raxaul, Ishwaree was flanked by Dharma Bahadur and the *Brahmachari*. She felt an unprecedented sense of contentment and happiness sitting so close to Dharma Bahadur.

God, she thought, had given her this opportunity. She felt that the key to happiness and contentment lay in her hands at this moment. Her heart trembled with passion and excitement. This was her chance — yes her chance for a lifetime of bliss. Someone seemed to whisper in her ear, "Such a chance will never come again. Grab it!"…The door to a new life was about to open for her. All the tortures that had plagued her since her husband's death would disappear. Very soon she would know whether he too agreed with her.

She saw, and was aware, that the paddy fields had become gilded by the golden tinge of the late afternoon sun. She saw that the crowds were getting thicker and that some families had come on *'tangas'* too. Almost all of them had a goat with them and some of these snuggled into the warm laps of the women, just as children seek the warmth and protection of their mothers. But how were they to know that they were seeking protection from the very people who were leading them to the sacrificial altar — that they were being led to their death?

She saw a river and wondered whether it was the famous Dugdhamati river, sanctified by the cow, Kamdhenu, taking a dip here after giving her milk to King Janak's daughter, Sita. Or was it the sacred 'Gairaki' river, which was said to be one of the holiest places in which to perform the rituals for a father's death.

But Ishwaree was beyond all this now — she could not remember such things.

Small islands of sands were scattered here and there on the river, looking very much like slabs of meat on a butcher's table, and geese of many different colours were sitting in the heart of the river. But, she found that she could think of nothing, see or feel nothing. The only thing she was aware of, or could feel, was the presence of Dharma Bahadur. Indeed, his very breath seemed to blow on to her body. She felt that her body had become completely one with another body leaving no trace of herself! Ishwaree found that this unwonted emotion was both blissful and tortuous. So this, she thought, was love! But love, real love was beyond the physical body alone — it's abode was in the soul.

But then, what is the soul, the *atman*? Ishwaree had never been satisfied with any of the answers to this question. She had never been able to find any adequate answer.

Yet, at this moment all her thoughts, all her feelings were centered on her physical body alone... She felt as though she was about to topple into the heart of the flowing river, like the loose earth on the river bank falls into it. What was this river that so resembled the body? Every single part of her body, every single limb, was awake and tingling. Ah! what exquisite torture! Her breasts became taut with passion and pleasure! Ah! what intense, and pleasurable anguish!

The bus proceeded towards Birganj. The river meandered along, visible at one moment, then lost to sight again, appearing and disappearing according to its course. During one of its appearances she saw that someone had killed a goat on the shore, and had gathered its bloody meat on to the goat's skin.

How could anyone do such a thing, she wondered in distaste — collect the animal's meat on its own skin!

Ishwaree's eyes suddenly fell on the *Brahmachari sannyasi* from the Chaturbhuj Sri Ram *Mandir* on banks of the Baitarini, who was sitting on her left. She was sitting in the middle of the two men. Someone had told her that this *sannyasi* had spent ten years in meditation in a dark cave in the Vindhya mountains. She wondered whether he had been successful in attaining complete control over his physical body. It was surely not at all an easy thing to attain such complete victory of the spiritual over the physical? Here he was sitting close to her, with his body touching hers! She had not been aware of it, but she now realized that one of his arms was touching her arm, in fact, almost lying on it!

She was afraid that this *brahmachari* had known about her thoughts and emotions. After all such deeply devoted *sannyasis* were supposed to be all knowing, able to understand all that goes on in the hearts and minds of others. Then he must think that she was an immoral woman!

A depraved woman! A sinful woman!

She had met a *sannyasi* from Giribraj at the Chitrakut Ramayan Conference. He was all skin and bones, and his matted hair had taken on the colour of old fishing nets hung out to dry. He was always present at every place that sang Sri Ram's praises, or spoke of his greatness. So everyone called him "Hanuman *Sannyasi*." He used to live on a platform on the top of a tree.

Ishwaree had only been recently widowed at that time. So

she had been very restless, and had gone to seek blessings from this holy man sitting on the treetop. He had obliged and blessed her. What had surprised her was that she had actually felt more somewhat more stable after this. And it was from then that she had started to have a feeling of respect for and also a kind of curiosity about such holy men. Indeed, after that she had earned the blessings of many and diverse *sannyasis* and *sadhus* — at Uttar Kashi, at Ratnasagar, at Ujjain. And now there was this *sannyasi* from the shores of the Baitarini River, complete with matted locks, sitting next to her, his body touching hers!

He must know everything about her by now — all about the condition of her mind and heart and body, about the tumult in her body! What must he think of her! He must be wondering why a woman like her had come to a religious meet like the Ramayan Conference.

But what was she to do? One single thought, one single feeling, had pushed everything else out of the way, and taken possession of her mind and body.

She had become entirely absorbed by Dharma Bahadur. There, one of his hands were resting on her thigh! She was too nervous, too emotional, to be able to look at it.

Their bodies seemed to have become words. No other vocal words were necessary. This Dharma Bahadur, who had been silent so long, now spoke to her — said all he needed to say, through his bodily touch. His physical touch said everything she had been so ardently hoping to hear, waiting to hear, at the many conferences at Chitrakut, Ujjain, and at Ayodhya.

Ah, there was such beauty and torture in this physical touch and mingling! A ring rubbed against her knees. What ring was he wearing? The hand continued to slide along her thigh, moving from one place to another! The ring rubbed against her again and again. It was as though the sand domes of some mountain river were sliding gradually and slowly down into the river. It seemed to her that, with immense self control, Dharma Bahadur, stopped himself from exploring further — that he willed himself to go just thus far and no further.

And here was the *sannyasi* from Baitarini sitting next to them. The foul smell of his matted hair assailed her nostrils!

It seemed to her that, on one side of her was a rough, unfeeling desert. And on the other side? A delightful grove, watered by benign and heavenly rain! On one side an ancient fortress destroyed and ravaged by war — and on the other side a glittering and illuminated liquor bar. This *sannyasi*, sitting in such close proximity to her, had come to know everything!

Again she felt the ring rubbing against her knee.

What was this ring that Dharma Bahadur was wearing — her Dharma Bahadur Rana? This ring that rubbed against her again and again? It was growing dark and gradually darkness covered the world.

Ishwaree's dreamlike trance was abruptly broken by a huge disturbance. All the passengers were shouting with one voice, "We have taken the wrong road! This is not the way to Birganj and Raxaul!"

All the lights of the bus were turned on at the same time and the interior of the vehicle lit up.

A hand, and the steel ring it was wearing, became clear. The light inside the bus was so bright! And this bright light pierced her very heart with a sharp dagger.

It was not Dharma Bahadur who was wearing the ring. It was the *sannyasi* — the *sannyasi* from the banks of the sacred Baitarini River!

The dagger that came with the light pierced deeper into Ishwaree's heart!

# PARASU PATOR'S WELL

It was a difficult choice for Parasu. His friends, those unemployed youngsters with whom he had spent hours gossiping beneath the big banyan tree at the Lakhimpur crossing, had disappeared one by one. Their disappearance was no mystery to Parasu. In fact, he had half a mind to join them. He knew the deep jungles where they were being trained in the use of arms and in warfare. But he had an ailing younger brother and his mother to take care of.

His friends had tried their best to persuade him. Money for his brother's expensive treatment, they cajoled, would be no problem if he joined the outfit. When he refused they mocked him, and scorned him in turn, calling him a spineless coward. But he remained firm — he would not desert his family in its time of need to go underground.

Parasu had never been a good student, and could not even pass his matriculation examination. But he badly needed a job, and had run from pillar to post, desperately looking for some work.

Someone told him that it would be best if he could get contracts from the government. Not only would he be able to look after his family well, he would also be able to save some money. So he started making the rounds of the offices, not in Lakhimpur alone, but in Guwahati too — the PWD offices, the Sericulture Department, the Military Army Supply Department, and so on, scanning all the tender notices available.

Parasu was not a very impressive personality. In fact he was very ordinary — pale and inconspicuous, rather thin, with big round eyes which were meek and naive. In Guwahati he managed to get hold of an old bicycle without mudguards from a friend. He went to the offices riding on this, wearing his old shirt with torn sleeves, and thin, slippery, worn out rubber sandals, his heels touching the ground as he walked. Indeed his condition echoed that of late Padma Nath Gohain Barua, who had lived in No. 14 Pratap Chandra Chatterjee Lane, in Calcutta, almost a hundred years ago. Padma Nath Gohain Barua had once written, " I have no shoes. I wear my friend's torn ones when I go out. I have no second set of clothes, so I borrow my friend's clothes, and even a towel to bathe."

At last Parasu heard of some work, a contract that he could take up in the Sericulture Department. Immediately he started haunting the office of the Executive Engineer. Neither rain nor the scorching sun of July could deter him. He stood in front of the office day after day, tirelessly waiting for a chance to meet the officer. The people of the neighbourhood, the peons and 'chaprasis', the tea stall owners, and other vendors, came to know him. Some even made fun of him.

Three tenders were offered by private contractors to the Sericulture Department for building a net house — a '*jali ghar*'— for keeping cocoons. Of course, only one of the three got the contract. But though the sanctioned amount was eleven thousand rupees, only seven thousand had been spent. As soon as this news spread, many small time contractors made a beeline to the Director's office, trying to find out how the remaining four thousand would be utilized. Most of these people were poor, with neither the means nor the power to test each other's worth. Sometimes they came face to face in a tea stall or a *paan* shop. But they were too embarrassed of their tattered sandals and shirts, which had been mended many times, to talk freely to each other. This however did not stop them from boasting about their lucrative contracts of lakhs of rupees in the past, or from letting the others know that this four thousand rupees contract was, in fact, a trifle for them!

Parasu sat under the big banyan tree in the compound of the Executive Engineer's office. Sweat poured down his back and his parched throat ached. He had eaten nothing since morning, and he was starting to feel the pangs of hunger. But he could not afford to risk going out to eat and thus maybe lose his chance. He had heard that the Additional Deputy Superintendent (ADS) usually came out of his room around this time to stretch his legs on the long veranda. There were such a lot of people! The veranda became overcrowded. People came and went. Some left with disappointed faces, some went with hope and joy writ large on their faces. Others stood waiting on the veranda, torn between hope and despair.

It was almost two o'clock. The scorching heat of the summer afternoon was intolerable, and Parasu's body seemed to shrivel up like the dried fibre of the *bhol* (gourd). Would the ADS not come out at all today? Parasu saw a gentleman passing by and asked, "Sir, what is the time?"

"Past two," came the reply.

"Past two? Then the officer will not come out today," Parasu sighed.

He wiped his forehead with his torn shirt sleeves. Suddenly he saw that the officer he was waiting for was sitting in his usual place in the wooden chair. Parasu had become familiar with the stout balding figure, right down to his shining shoes. He could even make out the large mole on his thick nose!

Without warning, Parasu shouted, " He has come! He has come! There he is!"

The ADS stood up. Parasu almost jumped, so overwhelmed that he didn't know whether to go down on his knees or to grasp the man's hands! The ADS yelled out in shocked surprise, "What do you want? Why are you behaving like this?"

"*Saar*, the left over money, *saar*?" said Parasu almost incoherent in his excitement.

"What money?"

"*Saar*, the money left over from the *'jali ghar'*."

"Oh, I see. You are talking about the money that was left over from that contract? The proposal that a well should be dug at Laimekuri with that money is out already. No, we have not taken any decision about that yet. And so many contractors have been here since this morning enquiring about it."

"We are very poor people, *saar*. I have a brother who is taking chemotherapy treatment at the Kalapahar Cancer Hospital in Guwahati, *saar*," Parasu beseeched, overcome with emotion, wiping the tears from his eyes.

The corpulent ADS, whose neck was almost hidden by excess fat, jumped back, as if Parasu's touch would pollute him. With a savage scowl, he asked, "What's your name?...Oh, yes, I have seen you hanging around here for the last one month. Your name?"

"Parasu Pator, *Saar*."

"Your bicycle is proof enough of your condition. You cannot even afford to repair the mudguard, and you come to construct a well at Laimekuri!"

"I am in deep trouble, *saar*. My brother's chemotherapy..."

"All right, all right! I understand. But I do not think you can even afford to pay the earnest money. Making a tubewell can somehow be managed; those rates were revised in 1999. But the rates for sanitary works and water supply are still the same as those of 1984. Even if you do get the contract, you will get the old rates which are less than the new ones. However, I cannot promise you anything now. I know nothing about the tender calls." Another group of contractors had surrounded the ADS.

Parasu did not rest assured with the half promise of the officer. He went to Gogamukh, and made a bid for a contract for repairing the farm house for the Sericulture Department, spending eight rupees and twenty five paise on stamp paper. But that is another story.

When he heard that he had got the contract for the Laimekuri well, Parasu could hardly believe his own ears! He did not know whether to laugh or to cry. He remembered how his friends, Dipakjyoti, and Paban, had scorned him and ridiculed him for not having the guts to join their outfit. Disappointment and frustration apparently had led them to enlist in ULFA, the United Liberation Front of Assam. They had gone to Charaipung for training, and then had continued through dense, almost impenetrable jungles to Kachin. Once Parasu had seen his friend, Bhola, hiding in the thick undergrowth of the tall *birina* grass near the paddy fields. He was with Bakul. Everyone in Lakhimpur knew about the love affair between Bhola and Bakul. Oh yes, everyone knew about it! Parasu could see Bakul's lovely white body and her thick silky hair. Her shimmering marble white figure seemed to illuminate the grass around her. What were these two doing? Were they kissing…? Or was Bhola trying to persuade her to take up arms? After all, some girls too had joined the outfit. Had not Parboti, also from Lakhimpur, gone all the way to Kachin to learn warfare?

Parasu loved Bakul deeply. But he never had the chance to tell her that. And he knew that he would always carry the sorrow of his unexpressed and unrequited love in his heart.

At the sight of Parasu, Bhola pushed the girl away from his arms and shouted, "Hey, Parasu! Come with me to Charaipung. If you do not, I tell you, your grandchildren too will be paupers like you. Come, come, do not be a coward."

Parasu immediately turned and walked rapidly away towards the high open grassland. But Bhola came after him leaving the girl in the tall grass. "Parasu," he said, "why should a capable young boy like you run here and there looking for a job? Here hold this." He thrust the shining gun into Parasu's hands.

Parasu saw Bhola clearly — the frightful marks of the elephant leech on his legs, the deep cut on his young cheek. The Indian Army that had come to fight against the underground outfit had blown off the lower part of Bhola's chin. Or had he hurt himself while training at Kachin? Parasu could not be sure. Bhola had whispered many things — many enticing, tempting things... And he was often tempted.

But how could he go? Damodar and their mother had to spend a lot at the Kalapahar hospital. Damodar's hair had fallen out due to the chemotherapy, and he was embarrassed to go out among other people. He simply sat at home refusing to see anyone or do anything, and not talking to anyone. Whatever meagre amount their mother earned working in the paddy fields was all spent on the boy's treatment. Their uncle in Guwahati was trying for some Government aid, but nothing had happened so far. So, young as he was, Parasu knew he had the terrible burden of responsibility. How then could he simply disappear like his luckier friends? Realizing that his friend was still unconvinced, Bhola shouted, "Shameless coward! Go then and become a slave of the government!" And he went his way.

Parasu met Chakradhar Mondal of Lakhimpur on the veranda of the Executive Engineer's office. Well built, robust and stylish, Mondal was dark, sharp nosed, and sported a thick moustache. His well-oiled hair was combed to resemble petals adorning his forehead. He was wearing a loose shirt, a *dhoti*, the front part of which was neatly pleated and tucked into his shirt pocket, and a pair of canvas shoes. In his hand was an umbrella.

"Parasu, I hear that you are in luck. Is that correct? If you could have signed the K2 form, you could have got a lot of things from the department, like iron and steel. But of course the Sericulture Department is not rich like the PWD. So you will not get any advantage or help there. By the way, the rates for sanitary works have not been revised since 1984. You need to be aware of this since your well construction work will fall under this category. I hear too that your contract falls under the heading of repairs of the Gogamukh farm house. Is that so?"

Parasu nodded. Chakradhar Mondal looked at him with a sly smile and said, "Parasu, you are trying to do something beyond your means. You will need at least six to seven thousand rupees immediately, plus all sorts of other things including rings for the well. Besides, you will get labourers only from the Mising tribe, and these tribal workers demand daily wages and good food. They are very poor people, and will accept nothing else."

Parasu looked helplessly at him. Clasping his hands in desperation, he said, "*Kokai*, you know everything. You know about my brother's condition; you know how our family was almost ruined after Deuta's death. Even our small paddy field had to be given out to sharecroppers."

"Parasu, you don't have to tell me all that," replied the wily Mondal. "You may be facing hard times now, but your family background is good. I am sure your mother still has some valuable pieces of old jewellery with her."

"No, no," said the near desperate young man. "Ma has nothing left. Damodar's illness has completely ruined us, *Kokai*. You must tell me what to do, you have helped many others like me…"

Gently patting his carefully coiffed hair, he said, "I can ask Rahmat Pathan for a loan. But he will demand some jewellery as security."

"I will ask Ma if she can help," Parasu replied.

"In that case there will be no problem," said Chakradhar Mondal encouragingly.

Mondal took Parasu to Sauldhowa ghat to meet Rahmat Pathan. Rahmat's power and influence in the Jonai sub division — including Laimekuri, Gogamukh and several *bastis* on the bank of the Dikhari River — was supreme. Besides, he had a large following of strong young men at his beck and call.

Rahmat Pathan Kabuliwala sat in state on a wooden chair in front of a tent on the banks of the Dikhari river. Sitting cross-legged on the ground near him was one of his trusted henchmen. Rahmat Kabuliwala had learnt to speak Asomiya fluently. He was very tall, nearly six feet, and broad shouldered. Parasu had never seen such a face before, with a rich, florid complexion, the colour of a ripe *'thekera'* fruit, blue eyes, red eyebrows, a long sharp nose and the black mark on his forehead, and the strange beard with various colours. He could not make out whether the beard was naturally that strange hue or whether it had been dyed red!

"Parasu," said Mondal, "show Pathan babu the *'thurias'*," referring to the indigenous and valuable Asomiya ear ornaments that Parasu's mother had given him. But the Kabuliwala was not too pleased. "What work can this skinny and underfed boy do? He looks so weak — one small jerk and he will fall flat on his face. I cannot lend him any money," he declared.

Mondal pleaded, "Rahmat Pathan, at least see the piece of jewellery he has brought." Pathan's servant looked scornfully at Parasu and burst into mocking laughter. Parasu was aghast! Was he really so thin and haggard, so useless looking?

"I have seen all your Asomiya jewellery, your *'thurias'* and *'gejeras'*, *'biris'* and *'kerus'*— I have seen them all."

"Surely then Rahmat *bhai*, you must have noticed that our jewellery is made from pure unadulterated gold, no fourteen, sixteen or eighteen carat for us. Only the purest gold is used for all our ornaments. Long ago, King Rudra Singha had sent a number of Kalita families to Benares to learn the art of jewellery making. At that time many of the lower castes like the Keots, Kochs, and even some of the Harias who normally deal with dead bodies, were promoted to Saikias and Hazarikas, after learning the art."

Rahmat Pathan laughed out loud and long. Parasu could see one golden tooth shining among the other black stained teeth. And in his pocket, wrapped carefully in a handkerchief, was the last piece of his mother's jewellery!...

His mother had displayed no emotion whatsoever while handing them out to him, but Parasu knew what it must have cost her, as if a part of her flesh had been torn out from her body. Yet she merely said, "Parasu, remember I have full faith in you. I know that you will be able to bring these *thurias* back in due time."

Parasu had asked, "Ma, Damodar will soon have to go to Guwahati again for his chemotherapy. What if I cannot finish the work by then?"

But his mother had scolded him in reply, "Have I not told you not to worry? I will start my herbal medicine business again."

"No, no, you must not!" burst out her son. "All that hunting around for leaves and herbs and roots, all that rubbing and squeezing to extract their fluids! You are not fit enough to do all that now. Tell all those people with blood dysentery to go to the hospital! Why, even drawing a single bucket of water from the well makes you sick and dizzy. Your hands and feet tremble. You must not start all that herbal medicine stuff again," he shouted in anguish.

Finally the shrewd words of Mondal convinced the moneylender. But he said, "I doubt whether this pair of earrings will be worth even a thousand rupees. But all right, I will give you five thousand at the usual rate of interest. Remember that you have to repay the debt with interest after one and a half months. Do not come and give me lame excuses later on."

"What are you saying, Pathan Babu? You know that I am on very good terms with the ADS and the Executive Engineer. Getting the bill passed will be no problem at all," Mondal replied on Parasu's behalf.

Returning along a narrow path through the sal, timber forest, Parasu looked at the beautiful orchids blossoming on the trees. But his mind was elsewhere. He now understood the truth of what his mother had so often said, "Words are the yardstick. Words have the power to make and also to break." Listening to the shrewd words of the crooked Mondal today, Parasu realized how wise his mother was. Would he himself ever learn to talk like that, he wondered? Impossible!

Parasu knew that his mother often wiped tears from her eyes when she thought nobody could see her. Everyone knew why she had been feeling sick lately, why her hands and feet trembled constantly. The message that every line of her forehead, every shiver of her body gave, was clear to all.

A peculiar smell had come from the tobacco - smoking Pathan's clothes. Parasu could hardly bear it. Indeed, at this moment, the man looked more like a butcher than anything else!

Chakradhar Mondal proved to be very helpful. He went to Laimekuri with Parasu, and helped him to recruit some local labourers — two Mising and four Bihari men at forty rupees each. He also organized the many things necessary for the construction of the well. Parasu decided that he would cook for all of them himself as it would be much cheaper. Also, he was quite used to cooking. Since Damodar's illness, he had often done the cooking at home.

The overseer had already marked out the site for the well: a little to the north of Laimekuri, near a small forest of *som* trees. These trees were important there, as it was on these trees that muga silk cocoons were reared. There, Parasu and his labourers prepared to offer a *puja* to the water god, the *'Jal Devta'*. For this auspicious occasion, Parasu had put on a clean shirt and pyjamas. But his feet were still shod in the same worn out, down-at the-heel rubber sandals. The strain of the last few days when he had been obliged to run around getting the many tasks completed had taken its toll on him. He was much thinner and his clothes hung loosely on his emaciated body. His cheek bones had become more prominent in his hollowed dried up face, and his untrimmed hair fell to his neck. He himself carried the cane basket with the items for the *prasad* on his head while in his shirt pocket were some packets of *dhoop* sticks *agarbattis*.

As they approached the site, Parasu saw that some people were already gathered there. The Mising labourers explained, "The children are probably here for the *puja*, and particularly the *prasad* — they always come when a new well is being dug."

But as they came nearer, Parasu was surprised to see that the crowd comprised of grown men, and not merely children as they had thought, and each one of them carried a stick in his hands. He foresaw trouble and stopped. The labourers too, with their tools and equipment, stopped short behind him. The villagers raised voices could be distinctly heard even from thirty yards away. "Hey, go back! This land belongs to the two brothers, Brikodar and Sahodar. The Sericulture department forcibly and illegally requisitioned much of their land for the department's farm. Let the law first decide the matter. We will not allow anyone to dig a well here before that. Go away!"

Parasu was not a brave man. He trembled with fear when he heard the loud and rough voices shouting at him. The two Mising labourers however said to him, "Come on, let us go forward. Do not be afraid, we will be right behind you." But Parasu hesitated.

The angry crowd roared, "Advance even two steps, and it will be us who will dig the well and bury you in it!" Parasu turned tail and fled, the labourers following close behind him. That was not the end of it either. The village children emerged from wherever they had been waiting, like bees erupting from a broken hive, and chased them, shouting in glee, "Leave your *prasad* behind. We want the *prasad*." Parasu hastily dropped the basket he was still carrying on his head, and the children fell on it like a swarm of flies.

After a couple of days, the overseer himself came and marked out another site to the west of the *som* plantation. Again, on an auspicious day, Parasu propitiated the *Jal Devta*, and the labourers started digging. This time there was no obstruction from the villagers. But they had dug about two feet deep when rocks and sand filled the hole. The well rings would not go down either.

The next day, Parasu himself went down into the hole with the labourers. But nothing would make the rings go down. After a while he looked up. And there was Rahmat Pathan's turbaned head peering down at him! A shiver of fear coursed through Parasu's body. He did not know what to do, and simply stood where he was, his body covered in a layer of mud from head to toe.

Rahmat Pathan yelled down at him, "What do you hope to do down there for? There are only mountains of stone and rocks there. Come up. And remember, you must repay the debt within two months."

Meanwhile, the old and the young of Laimekuri had gathered there. They too agreed with the Pathan. "He is right," they said, "So many parties have come here to dig wells but all have gone back frustrated. And look at this skinny boy trying to dig a well here!" And they burst into scornful laughter.

The words pierced Parasu like a knife. But he resumed

digging, undeterred. Sparks flew as his spade hit the rocks, but he continued. After two days of relentless digging the stones became even tougher. Once again, looking up, Parasu saw the Kabuliwala's threatening eyes. But he pretended not to see him and went on digging. He heard someone say, "What a fool! Six rings have already broken and he still digs on!"

"The devil has got into him!"

"Come up boy, come out before it is too late."

Both the Mising and Bihari labourers soon became tired of digging and lifting heavy rocks and sand from the well.

Again someone shouted, "*Jodha murkha*! Idiot! Don't you know that three parties of well diggers came here and could do nothing? This is a cursed place haunted by the *Jal Devta* himself. You can hear him come here at midnight, rowing a boat, and drawing water in a pitcher from a well. Fool! You can't dig a well in Laimekuri."

The mud-smeared Parasu shouted up, "Just wait and see! I will show you! I will dig a well here in this very place, and show you!"

After the seventh ring broke, the Bihari labourers climbed out panting. A big mound of sand and stone had formed on the ground beside the well. The children from the village were having great fun playing there. Parasu too climbed up, and sat dejected for some moments. None of them had eaten anything since morning, and it was now late afternoon. Everything for the meal was ready. His mother had carefully sent all the necessary items — the utensils, rice, *dal*, potatoes, and even some delicious *Khaarali chutney*, made from mustard seeds and soda powder, wrapped in banana leaves. Parasu was supposed to have come up from the well and cooked the meal while the labourers worked. But now, the midday sun and the heaps of rock and sand seemed to mock him. He had neither the desire nor the strength to cook.

At this moment, the oldest man of Laimekuri arrived at the site looking for his cattle which had wandered away. He looked at the dejected Parasu and said encouragingly, "Go to the overseer my boy and ask him to find another site for the well. Why do you punish yourself in vain?"

But Parasu remained defiant and obstinate. "I will dig the well here!" he declared. "I will bring out clear sweet water and show you all. *Kokai*, please do not discourage me."

One day, as he was passing through the *som* forest on his way to the overseer's office, Parasu happened to see Rahmat Pathan. The Kabuliwala probably had some other debtors in the area, but the very sight of the moneylender filled him with such dread that both the mounds of rock and sand heaped beside the half dug well, as well as his own emaciated body appeared like corpses over which the Pathan hovered like a vulture closing in on its prey. Parasu trembled in fear, but Rahmat Pathan went his way without even glancing at him.

In the afternoon the overseer came, dressed in a flowery bush shirt and shorts. He surveyed the half dug well, and the rocks and domes of sand alongside. Pointing at these he asked, "What is all this? What is happening? You should have stopped at five feet and informed us. But you have dug upto ten feet! The department cannot pay you for the loss..."

"*Saar*", Parasu entreated, "six of my rings broke. As they say in the proverb, *the seed has become longer than the actual vegetable.* The main job has remained undone, while these side jobs are piling up until they are now bigger than the actual work. Help me, please sir help me."

Another old man looking for his cows came up and said, "Come my son, don't cry. Babu will help you; just give him a good warm *endi chaddar*, or some such gift."

The villagers gathered around roared with laughter. The overseer scowled and looked around. "You pack of fools!" he said, "You should have told me about the sand and the stones you found as soon as you had dug two feet deep." He climbed down the well and surveyed the ruin there – of sand, rocks and broken rings.

But before he left the site, he and Parasu must have come to some mutual understanding...

Once again, on his way home with the labourers, Parasu met the kabuliwala cycling back from some nearby village. The Pathan almost growled at him, "I hope your work is progressing well, Parasu. Or are you still digging out just rocks and sand?"

Parasu merely nodded. But to anyone observing him, his thin haggard face spoke volumes, expressing many unspoken thoughts and emotions.

Sailabala, Parasu's mother, had heard of a holy man, a water diviner, who was doing the rounds of the nearby villages. She met him and sent him to Laimekuri.

He was known as *'Paani Baba'* (the water man). Though thin and weak with age, he went around with a long Y shaped stick in hand, piercing the ground with its pointed lower part, hunting for, and finding water in many dry villages. In that open space in the middle of the forest too he crawled around on the ground armed with his wondrous stick, listening carefully with his ears to the ground. The children crowded around him in wonder and curiosity. It was said that this holy man with his tangled hair, saffron *dhoti* and a '*Ramnami*' *chador*, with the names of the gods printed on it, had the power of divining water even in hard, dried up soil. He had been successful on most occasions, but this was a cursed part of land, cursed by the *Jal Devta* himself! Would *Paani Baba* succeed here? If he failed what would happen to Parasu?

Suddenly *Paani Baba* stopped and stiffened. Then he somersaulted three times in the air. Laughing, he rang the bell he carried, and shouted, "Dig here. If water does not come out at this spot, my name is not *Paani Baba*. Dig, dig! Bring out the *Jal Devta*, bring him!"

The children following him also shouted repeating his words gleefully.

The Sericulture department, however, ruled out a well so far from their farm. And nothing, not all the pleadings and entreaties of Parasu could move the officers to reconsider their decision.

The overseer came again and pointed out another site between the two villages. He was adamant and would listen to no one. The well must be dug exactly where he wanted. He even marked out a well six feet in diameter. And that was that!

This time Parasu did not even think of propitiating the Gods — he was too engrossed in thoughts of his brother. Damodar's condition had deteriorated, and the harsh chemotherapy was affecting him badly. The very thought brought tears to his eyes. Had he done the right thing in borrowing all that money for the well when his brother needed him so badly? Should he have joined his friends — Moina, Haibor, Jogesh, and gone to Charaipung? Maybe he should have. At least there would have been no dearth of money for Damodar's treatment. Their mother would have been saved a lot of trouble and heartache. Maybe...

This time the work proceeded smoothly as planned. After digging about five feet, they started putting in the rings. After three rings went in easily, the labourers shouted in joy. For one week, Lady Luck was on their side. But trouble started with the tenth ring. It would not move! Parasu went down on his knees inside the temporary shed and started praying, silently and secretly.

Meanwhile, inside the well, the labourers noisily tried everything they knew. There could be some tough roots of old plants entwined in the mud — who knew where the long, twisted roots went? Just as no one could tell whose skull and bones were scattered where in a cemetery. After all, old bones and old roots were similar in colour, so why not in behaviour too! So the labourers toiled away, hacking here, digging there, in a vain attempt to set the well rings in place.

As Parasu sat alone propitiating the Gods, he heard a gruff voice behind him. He jumped up in alarm and turned around. It was not the *Jal Devta*, , but Rahmat Pathan standing ominously in front of him, leaning against his bicycle.

"I am watching you, Parasu," he roared. "I don't see much hope that you will be able to complete your well. Remember that you must repay your loan soon. You even signed the papers. Everyone knows how I function."

Parasu went numb with fear. He tried to say something, but the Kabuliwala disappeared down the lane as suddenly as he had appeared.

The labourers went on with their digging and pulling but to no avail. The rings would go down a little further, and then would get stuck again.

It was getting late. The labourers climbed out frustrated and called it a day. They had to go all the way to Jonai for the night. Parasu did not get up. He simply said, "You can all go now. Come early tomorrow morning. I will stay here for some time."

"How can you stay here all alone?" they said. "The place is full of wild animals."

"A group of *Bhaona* performers will be passing this way from Lakhimpur. I have asked them to bring news of Damodar. So I will have to wait for them."

A lovely clear moonlight transformed the entire landscape. The paddy fields and the forests around shone with a pale, ethereal light. The trees and shrubs looked unusually clean, as though someone had come and polished them with a piece of old, smooth silk just moments ago. The sand particles glistened like silver in the mound beside the well. The schoolmaster of Laimekuri had said that he would take all the sand to fill up the land around his house, but he had not come so far. To Parasu's melancholy mind, sometimes the pieces of broken rock amidst the silvery sand looked like dried up old bones left over from some funeral pyre!

After some time, he saw the group of actors in the distance.

They were a happy lot, apparently without a care in the world! Marigold garlands around their necks, they were talking cheerfully in loud voices.

Parasu called out, "Is that Sonabaap and Haladhar?"

They shouted back, "Parasu is that thing lying there like a dead elephant your well?"

"Come, come nearer, and you will see it all in the moonlight."

"Oh yes," one of them replied, "We can see it now. We have been wandering around like lost souls!"

"Be careful", cautioned Parasu. "There are some of those itchy *'bandorkekoa'* plants on one side."

They came and surrounded Parasu. "We heard that you were having a really tough time with the well?"

Most of them had been in very high spirits, singing and dancing as if they did not have a care in the world. But at the question, they fell silent. Haladhar spoke, "Listen Parasu, the news is not good but don't lose heart. Damodar suddenly fainted as he was having lunch. He was taken to Guwahati today. The doctors cannot tell why he fainted without examining him."

Parasu felt as if his heart was breaking — he could not utter a word. The short and stocky Haladhar grasped his friend's hands in sympathy and said, "Your mother asked me to tell you not to worry. Your uncles are in Guwahati, and they will do the needful. Now go back to Jonai before it gets too late."

Walking back to Jonai on this moonlit night, alone with his thoughts, Parasu trippd many times over the rough fields, his sad mind filled with thoughts of Damodar. Would his little brother die — his beloved little brother, with whom he had grown up playing and quarrelling? He could not bear the thought of it.

The guava trees were tinged by the moonlight, and the lower parts of the tree trunks resembled marble structures. But Parasu saw only darkness and doom. The clods of earth scattered in the paddy fields seemed like the helmets of dead soldiers in a battlefield. It was as if everything, nature itself, was conspiring to drag him into some unknown dreaded cavern! And grimly watching all this was the butcher-like money lender, Rahmat Pathan!

Early next morning the labourers again started their work. But try as they might, the rings could not be moved. The two Mising men struggled for three back-breaking hours, but the rings could not be budged. "What a cursed land this is", they cried. "We cannot carry on like this anymore, we cannot." They climbed out of the half dug well.

Parasu who was busy cooking their meal reared up like a struck cobra. Without a word, he changed into a loincloth, left his cooking, and went down into the well. He started scraping the edges of the rings very carefully. For three hours he struggled tirelessly and alone, working like a madman. Then suddenly he felt a strong root touch his hands — a root as thin as a lizard's tail. He was elated, and felt like turning three somersaults inside the well! He started pulling at the root with renewed energy but it was lodged so deeply that he could do nothing with it. One of the Mising labourers climbed down to help him, and between them they managed to pull the root into view. The children who were looking on curiously chanted gleefully in unison, "Pull, pull! Pull out the monkey's tail! Pull!"

The Mising boy climbed out and brought a large *dao*, and this time the Bihari men too climbed down with him. But they simply could not pull out the entire root; it was stuck so fast in the mud. They had to be very careful — one false stroke and the rings would crack. They climbed out again.

After a while they went down again and chopped away at the root with the *dao*, piece by piece. What had looked like a thin lizard's tail in the beginning, became bigger and thicker as more and more of it emerged out of the soil. A peculiar milky substance oozed out from the gashes caused by the *dao*. It was amazing! No one had ever seen anything like it before. Who could tell how deeply the root was embedded in the earth! Or was it the rope used by the *Jal Devta* himself to draw water from his well? Another stroke of the *dao*, and suddenly the diggers were drenched in a thick blood-like liquid. Within minutes, the rings started going in and fitting into their slots without any problem. From a distance, the village girls on their way to fetch water from the Laimekuri public well could be heard singing, propitiating the *Jal Devta* for good sweet water.

One by one the rings went down fitting in neatly and smoothly. The labourers shouted in joy. For a week the work proceeded without a hitch. Fifteen rings were fitted inside the well, but there was no sign of water. The driver of the schoolmaster's bullock cart, who had at last come to collect the stones, sand and other unwanted material gave his verdict, "When there is no water even after fifteen rings, there is no hope. Many have tried here before and failed."

Instead of water, the labourers brought out bucket after

bucket of silt, and red and black mud, the likes of which had never been seen before. Someone commented that he hoped the place had not been a graveyard or crematorium in the distant past. If it had, no one would touch the water, even if by some chance water was found. Parasu scrutinized bucket after bucket of the mud, but fortunately could not find any tell-tale pieces of bones.

Again, from somewhere, came floating the voices of the girls singing the praises of the *Jal Devta*, beseeching and propitiating him.

Gradually the silt laden black soil gave way to wet mud. Parasu, who had never dug a well before, became hopeful. Perhaps at long last he was close to water. He went on digging like a man crazed. The Mising labourers remarked, "You may look thin and weak but you have the strength of an elephant!"

Eighteen rings went down but only damp sand came out. Again Parasu seemed to hear the song of the village girls, "*Jal Devta, Jal Devta,* have mercy. Open your eyes; we pray to you, and propitiate you with flowers and garlands; Lord have mercy..."

Wonder of wonders! Three days later, clean clear water gushed out and filled almost a quarter of the well. It was as if the water Gods were sporting with Parasu, testing his grit and perseverance. He now became even more desperate, like a thirsty man chasing a mirage in the desert. He must complete the well...

Suddenly, one day, without any kind of warning the waist deep water in the well dried up! The Mising labourers climbed out of the well in fright and refused to go back. Even the braver Biharis refused to go down despite the pleadings of Parasu. The villagers gathered around shouted, "Come up, come up. We have never seen anything like this before! Come back up."

But Parasu paid no heed to all this. Alone, he dug up bucket after bucket of mud. The people were amazed at his perseverance and strength. Once when he happened to look up, he thought that he saw a man in a turban watching him. That must be the Kabuliwala waiting to claim his pound of flesh.

He did not ask the Misings to go down the well again to help him. He alone would dig and bring up the water. If anyone were to die in the process, he would be the one.

There would be no end to his troubles if one of the labourers were to get hurt or die. The Department would demand that he compensate from his own pocket. He remembered the case of the two labourers who had died in the Rangajuli well when poisonous gas had leaked out. The contractor had become almost bankrupt after paying the compensations. No, he would not risk anything of that sort. He would dig the remaining portion of the well himself with no other help!

The area around the well site became crowded with inquisitive people from around Laimekuri. They gazed at him in wonder as if he were some rare animal at the zoo! Rahmat Pathan was also there for a long time, his turban conspicuous in the crowd of villagers, the top part of it fanning like a hooded cobra, waiting to strike at Parasu!

Water appeared once more in the well, but even after a week's strenuous digging, it was no more than about three feet deep. Parasu worked on tirelessly. One day the Supervisor came cycling all the way from Jonai, wearing a pair of shorts with no less than three fountain pens in his shirt pocket! He wore a pair of heavy framed spectacles and sported a luxuriant moustache. He was known throughout Laimekuri for his bad and violent temper.

Finding nothing better, he sat down on a bundle of firewood and asked Parasu to draw a bucket of water from the well to show him. He examined the water thoroughly, once with his spectacles on, and once, for good measure, without them! He was not satisfied, and Parasu had to draw three more buckets of water for him to examine. The Supervisor seemed to be in a dilemma! He could not decide whether the water was red or bronze in colour. Of course, there was no question of it being clean and clear.

He took a small box from his pocket, picked a *paan* with betel nut, laced with tobacco and lime, and chewed on it to help him make up his mind.

Parasu was sitting on the ground in front of the man, hopefully gazing up at his face. Some other inquisitive people, including the labourers and the driver of the schoolmaster's bullock cart were silently staring at this important man.

After a while the supervisor broke his silence, "You fool! This was not the site for the well! And you have dug deeper than the Department had permitted!"

Parasu did not utter a word. He just stood there in his wet half pants, his entire body covered in mud. His hands had been injured by the sharp rocks.

Again the supervisor roared, "I cannot, in any way, certify this to be clean and clear water. I can only give a certificate of red water. Look at this water, see for yourself... Is it clear and clean?"

He took some water from the bucket and threw it at Parasu.

Parasu sighed deeply. The bullock cart driver spoke up, "Sir, a red water certificate will ruin the boy. He will get no money at all." But the superintendent would not listen to him and went back the way he had come.

It had become a habit for the people of Laimekuri, both old and young, to gather at the site of Parasu's well every afternoon. They had all come to like the simple lad. They were sympathetic and helpful, impressed by the young man's determination and perseverance.

One of the Mising youths advised, " Parasu *kokai*, try pouring sand into the well. About two feet of sand might help to make the water clear." Others too thought it to be a good idea.

For three days thereafter sand was poured into the well. Parasu was more determined than ever to bring out clean water from his well. And indeed, after three days, the effect of the sand was obvious — the water actually changed colour. It was as though the source of this sparkling water was the Chandrabhaga river itself, flowing down from the pristine Himalayas!

Now Parasu — no, not just Parasu alone, but the labourers and all the inhabitants of Laimekuri too, waited hopefully for the supervisor to come and certify the water to be clean and pure. Whenever they saw anyone come their way on a bicycle, they shouted, "Here he comes, here he comes!" Some naughty children even made up a rhyme and chanted it whenever they spied a likely figure.

"Potted belly, whistling mouse,
The super comes hoosh, hoosh, hoosh!

Stomach fat with lots of bribes,

Jump three times and kick, kick,kick!"

When the supervisor failed to turn up even after three more days, Parasu lost patience. He filled a clean bottle with the sparkling water from his well and cycled down to the Jonai office with the bottle tied carefully to the cycle's handle.

The way to Jonai was beautiful with fragrant flowers all around. The clear, shimmering Dikhari river was full of silver trout that played about in the water. The entire atmosphere seemed to radiate joy and beauty. As he cycled along, Parasu heard a lilting joyous Mising Bihu song floating in from somewhere. He saw some of those brightly coloured little *'fesulika'* birds, the lovely little barbet birds, and the speckled woodpeckers. His heart was suddenly filled with hope and joy. No one, but no one, could now reject the clear water in his bottle!

Parasu had to wait again for three days for the supervisor. Sometimes he was told that he had gone to Guwahati, sometimes to Laimekuri. Seeing Parasu day after day with the bottle of water, the children took to teasing him, "Parasu's bottle is the Rai bahadur's car; He brings water – *sopong, sopong...*"

Parasu was in no way bothered by all this. He went around displaying his water to many in the Department, and all who saw it praised its quality. Rahmat Pathan too did not fail to see Parasu with his bottle of water tied to his bicycle.

Matters came to such a head that the Executive Engineer and the supervisor were compelled to go and examine the well. How at last the officers certified Parasu's water to be clean and good, and not red, is a long story. But it was doubtful that this certificate alone would guarantee payment of all the bills. Parasu realized that he would not get the full amount due to him. Besides, the frequent change of sites meant that he had had to spend a lot more than planned on labour charges. He had very little money left, and he was bitterly aware that he would not be able to retrieve his mother's earrings. Who knew what huge amount the Kabuliwala would demand, with his interest and all!

He first paid off his labourers and dismissed them. If he could get the bills cleared within a month, he might be able to give his mother at least some amount of money for Damodar's treatment. How he longed to see his brother!

He sat for a long time under the empty shed staring into the distance. The shed too would be pulled down the next day. The well was in front of him, the living symbol as it were of his harsh battle for survival. Damodar would have loved to see the well. No, he could not imagine a future — a world — without Damodar. His tortured mind could only think so far, and no further. Everything went blank after that.

As he sat alone pensively he was filled with sorrow. The pale moonbeams seemed to dampen the fallow land, just as the unshed tears dampened the very heart and soul of Parasu. His mind went back to the happier days of childhood. Damodar used to follow him everywhere like a shadow. Why did this have to happen to him, of all people! He could not bear even to think about it!

Damodar had never liked going to school, so Parasu used to carry him on his shoulders all the way. But the younger boy had turned out to be the better student. Once, Parasu remembered,

the school inspector had come to visit the school and Damodar
had been able to recite the names of all the books by that great
novelist, Rajani Kanta Bordoloi! He had even worked out three
sums absolutely correctly winning everyone's praise. The elders
of the village always said that Damodar was far above Parasu so
far as intelligence was concerned. Parasu, they said, would stay
with his mother and help in the matters of the household while
Damodar would grow up to be a *Bara Babu* (a Head Clerk).
What had gone wrong? Parasu suddenly remembered how his
younger brother had longed to wear rubber sandals.

Standing under a tall *silikha* tree, he pensively surveyed the
well he had dug. He thought it looked like a large kite lying on
the ground with its string torn — a useless thing!

He longed to see his brother and tears rolled down his cheeks.

Parasu went straight to Lakhimpur without bothering to
stop at the office in Jonai. There was still much to be done in
connection with the various official matters with regard to the
well, matters which had not even crossed his mind as he had
struggled against the rocks and sand deep inside the unfinished
well.

Now that he was done with that part of the work, his mind
became agitated and distressed. He realized that the Herculean
task of getting the government to clear his bills still lay ahead.
He also had yet to get the promised certificate of " pure, clean
water" in his hands. And, over and above all else, loomed the
ever present threat of Rahmat Pathan. But first of all he had to
go and see his brother, see him before it was too late.

He crossed the familiar landmarks almost without noticing

— the Diehard bridge, Silapothar, Gogamukh, Subansiri bridge at Saikhowa ghat. When finally he reached the vast open fields near his home in Lakhimpur, the scorching afternoon sun was shining mercilessly down on his bare head. All the way home thoughts of his dying brother had haunted him. Still, he had not been afraid as he walked on alone, because Rahmat Pathan did not hold sway over these parts. It was said that the Kabuliwala kept some Asomiya, Mising and Bihari *goondas* to help him in getting his debts paid. How could this heartless moneylender understand the torture in Parasu's mind? He had never been poor, so how could he understand that a life could be ruined, an entire family devastated by poverty. What after all was the meaning of life? Was it not but an endless and unattainable path, full of misunderstandings, and heart rending separations? All kinds of melancholy thoughts tortured his simple mind.

Suddenly he saw that a crowd had gathered near a ditch in the distance. Vultures were circling above a tall *jamun* tree near the ditch. Half running, half panting, Parasu reached the place. No one bothered to ask him about the well he had dug at Laimekuri — it was unimportant at this juncture. All were silent and still, their shocked eyes full of fear. Parasu pushed forward... Dear God! There was Bhola lying in a pool of blood, blood on his chest, and on his forehead. Ah! He was dead, shot through the heart. There was another dead body, a woman's body that someone had covered with a *chador*. Her shining, long black hair had become entangled in the clods of mud. Who was she? Could it be Bakul?

It had to be her. Bhola had come here quite often from

Charaipung to meet Bakul. Parasu had seen them together many times. Sometimes Bhola would call out to him from behind the bushes asking him to join them. Parasu would quickly move away, Bakul's laughter following him, the scornful laughter of the girl he had always loved.

Who had killed them, Parasu wondered? The village post master, Bhupen Bharali, came towards him, and beckoned to him to come aside. "Know what?" Bharali whispered. "They found the official documents with Bakul. It seems that she had been trying to bring Bhola back to the main stream. By the way, I heard that you have been digging a well at Laimekuri...?"

People thronged the place. Suddenly a police jeep arrived noisily on the scene and stopped some distance away. There was no motorable road going right up to the ditch. The crowd became restive. Parasu could not wait much longer; he did not have time to loiter. His head reeled with all that he had been through. He almost ran homeward. He could no longer tolerate the sight of the helpless dead figure of his friend. Where was his gun? Bakul's lifeless face haunted him all the way. Someone had put a bullet through her lovely young body, and she was gone forever. Once a person was dead, what did it matter who had struck her! After the body was burnt, one could not measure from the skull and the bones that remained how or why one person had struck the other, why one's very soul had been hurt. Such was life!

The villagers were still flocking to the ditch; the entire village seemed to have descended there. Parasu had been away for a month and a half, holed up inside the well. But today, none of the villagers were concerned with him, or even remembered about the well. He started panting. Once again, he was immersed in a well — a bottomless and frightening well that was made up of the ways of human life, a well that seemed to fill up with Bakul's beautiful black hair spread out to cover her lovely bosom. With such thoughts for company, haunted by pictures of the dead Bakul, he at last reached his home.

Parasu's mother and brother had returned from Guwahati just two days back. The doctors there had advised that Damodar should be taken to Vellore for further treatment.

This time, even his strong willed mother, Sailabala, who hailed from Gargaon, renowned for its strong and persevering women, had lost heart. She had become thin and pinched with worry and sorrow. Parasu could not bear to look at her face.

Damodar was no longer the boy he used to be. Even after seeing his beloved elder brother after such a long time he could not summon the strength to get up from his bed. He was too weak to even rejoice at his brother's return. After a while, he managed to sit up and lean against the wall. Pointing to a handmade fan stuck into the bamboo wall he said, "For you."

Sailabala joined in. "He made this fan from bits of bamboo before we went to Guwahati. But now he cannot even work with his hands…. He had a great desire to see your well."

Parasu did not reply. The horrifying murder he had seen on the way left him dumb. But at the same time he did not want to leave his brother's side.

That night, Chakradhar Mondal came and stood in their

courtyard.

"You saw what a terrible thing happened this morning, didn't you?" he said. "I was there too, and I saw Parasu coming this way. That is why I have come — to enquire about him."

Although Parasu had borrowed the money for his work from Rahmat Pathan, he did not have much respect for him. He had gradually come to realize that Mondal was as sly as a fox. He could stoop to anything for the sake of money and self – interest — from giving false witness to creating a rift between brothers over matters of landed property. Yet he was on such good terms with all the people who mattered — from political leaders to cheats and moneylenders, that the ordinary people of the village were compelled to seek his help in times of trouble. Noticing Damodar lying on his bed, Mondal said, "Now I understand why Parasu has come running to see his brother."

Sailabala replied, "I did not purposely tell Parasu about his brother's condition, knowing how important his work was."

"It is extremely difficult to get the government bills paid," said Mondal. "Who knows when the Executive Engineer will disappear, or when the accountant's mother will conveniently die! This is a very critical time, the time to sit on the office steps and wait to catch the concerned officers."

The ever hospitable Sailabala put the oil lamp on its stand in front of Mondal. She sat on the ground near it and offered him the traditional *tamul-paan*.

"I had somehow managed to persuade Rahmat Pathan to lend your son some money," he said. "He usually refuses to have anything to do with ordinary poor people. He agreed only because I intervened and almost begged him to help Parasu. He has reminded me that he wants the debt repaid within two weeks. It seems someone shot Pathan's brother dead. A number of non-Asomiya businessmen were killed too, and the Kabuliwala is in a terrible rage."

Parasu heard him, and coming out, sat close to his mother. He was still deeply affected by the morning's ugly incident. After a short silence he said, "This is a very bad time for us. I gave Ma's *thurias* as security only because I thought Damodar could be helped by it."

Mondal popped a *paan* into his mouth and said, "There is hardly any gold in those. No one else would have loaned five thousand rupees against them. Now you must repay Pathan as soon as you can clear your bills. He has been making enquiries."

Sailabala could not restrain herself. "We are in great trouble," she cried out, "great trouble."

Parasu said, "As you must be aware, we are passing through particularly bad times now. The Department gave me very little advance. Besides, the well site had to be changed, and that cost me a lot of money with the labourers. *Kokai*, you are like an elder brother to me. Do you know, a number of the rings broke into bits; it was a terrible and expensive waste. Now, the very thought of calculating the cost scares me."

Mondal's sly eyes glittered malevolently. His carefully oiled hair shone in the light of the lamp. He had a broad face and a thick nose. All in all, he was not a pleasant sight. "Come now, don't worry," he said. "I will help you with your calculations."

They sat down to the task in the lamp light. Mondal

calculated all the costs — the costs of the labourers, the rings, other tools and equipment, rations and so on. Everything was done methodically and efficiently. Sailabala went inside and got them two glasses of tea.

Even when they were absorbed in their calculations, they heard Damodar's tormented moans of pain. They could hear the sounds of Sailabala washing Damodar's hands and feet, and they also heard him vomiting. But Chakradhar Mondal was oblivious to the boy's intense suffering.

It was getting late; the beautiful moon seemed entangled in the leafy branches of the slim *bijulee* bamboo behind the shed where Parasu's mother pounded paddy with the *dheki*, the pounding pedal. The eerie howling of jackals could be heard in the distance, from the forest of sal trees.

Around this time, Sambhu Kumar, and Baliram, the high school chowkidar came to ask about Damodar. They sat outside in the small courtyard trying to talk about the morning's happenings to Mondal. But Mondal today had no time for anything else. He had come with the sole purpose of helping Parasu.

Sambhu and Baliram looked at the sleeping Damodar from the doorstep, and cried out in compassion, "He has become so thin, he has no flesh on his body at all. Parasu, you must make arrangements to take him to Vellore immediately."

Hearing this, Parasu got up to go to his brother. But Mondal caught hold of his hands forcing him to sit down again. The two guests turned their attention to Parasu and started praising him. " We heard that you have dug a well forty feet deep at

Laimekuri, and that you were inside it for three whole days, so absorbed in your work that you did not even think of eating or sleeping. Surely, with such rare  perseverance you will rise high in life. You will surely prosper,Parasu."

Sailabala came out of the hut wiping her tears. "We are in great trouble, in terrible danger," she wept.

Sambhu tried to console her, "Do not cry sister. God is merciful and he will deliver you from this trial also."

Baliram too echoed, "The ever merciful God will definitely come to your aid. *Baideo*, remember we are always here to help you in any way you want."

After a little while they took their leave, and Mondal too finished his work. All the calculations became crystal clear. Parasu had taken an advance of two thousand rupees, and he had spent ten percent on bribery. This ten percent Mondal showed as part of the cost of materials. Parasu was shocked at this blatant dishonesty, and was stunned into silence! Truly, he was very raw in such matters! But he doubted whether he himself would ever be able to use such trickery in any business deals.

Now he would have to bribe the accountant and the executive engineer with a bottle of whisky and a pair of good warm *endi* shawls each. After that, according to Mondal's calculations, Parasu would be left with a profit of about three thousand rupees.

Sailabala saw a ray of hope. Now perhaps they would be able to take Damodar to Vellore, and all would be well. In her elation she said to Mondal, "I have cooked some rice and *dal*. There is also some *khaarali chutney*. We would be happy if you dined here."

Mondal jumped up, shocked! "No, no. I never eat without bathing. Besides, I always recite some prayers before my meals."

Almost choking with emotion, the simple Sailabala said, "It is God's blessing that a good god-fearing person like you has befriended my son, and come to us as our saviour!"

Chakradhar had the grace to be embarrassed. Coughing awkwardly, he stood and spat out the betel nut juice. All three walked towards the bamboo pole that served as a gate. Suddenly Mondal stopped and said, "People usually give me a commission for arranging loans from Rahmat Pathan. There are instances when some have even given sufficient paddy to last for some years. However, being aware of your condition, I will not ask for much. But when you repay Pathan's debt, he will return the *thurias*. You can give me those as my commission. I doubt whether there is even five annas of gold in the pair, but it will be enough in your difficult situation. Of course I will pay something for it."

Parasu and his mother stood speechless, as if struck by a sudden thunder bolt! They had hoped that after paying the Kabuliwala and getting the earrings back, they would take more loans using them as security again. They stood rooted to the spot, overcome by shock and grief, while Mondal's footsteps faded into the distance.

Suddenly hearing Damodar vomiting, Sailabala ran inside. But Parasu did not move. Looking up, he saw some golden clouds in the night sky. To his distressed eyes, they seemed more like clods of earth hiding a slice of the moon, like the hooves of a dead horse in a battlefield!

When Parasu went to the office to get his bills cleared, he had to bear the brunt of a lot of complaints that had apparently been made against him. It appeared that the Director of Sericulture had gone to Laimekuri to inspect the well twice when Parasu was in Lakhimpur, as there had been some complaints. He was quite annoyed with Parasu because, according to him, Parasu should not have dug such a deep well at a site where the water level was so low. It was simply a waste of government money. The certificate however was given, and he was told the bill payment too would be made.

Parasu had to travel all the way to Guwahati, making the journey in two stages, in two different trucks, trying to locate the junior engineer. For three days he had gone without food, until he happened to meet one of his friends who had gone underground, and was now in disguise with a big moustache and dark glasses, trying to hoodwink the police. The two of them had a good meal of rice and mutton curry. Before leaving, the friend said, "Who are these officers that are skinning you alive? Just tell me their names, and I will blow their brains out…" Parasu was so scared that he could breathe freely only after he had come out from the restaurant and his friend had left!

He spent days and nights haunting the executive engineer's office, so much so that most people around came to know the story of his well. But that is another story…

Finally his bills were sanctioned, and he got the money, though less than Chakradhar Mondal had calculated.

That night, mother and son sat down again, engrossed in

calculations of a different nature. Sailabala had already met the old Haliram Burha Bhakat of their village, who had recently returned from Vellore .They calculated that it would not be possible to meet the expenses of Vellore after paying off the debt with the interest.

Sailabala sat weeping and dejected. Chakradhar Mondal must have already informed the Pathan that the bills had been cleared and that he had received the money. Parasu waited anxiously at the gate expecting to hear the Pathan's dreaded footsteps any moment. He had asked Mondal to tell Rahmat Pathan about Damodar's condition, but he did not really believe that Mondal would have said a word about it. After all, he suddenly realized, Mondal had not cared to even look at Damodar. *— Moment of epiphany*

Damodar had left his bed after one whole week, and had been able to come and sit outside. Now the hard-hearted, harsh Pathan would arrive at any moment, armed with sharp words, demanding money. The man would definitely come today, because Parasu knew that he had already collected his debts from others in the area, and now he was the only one left.

There was a hammering in his ears — *dhak, dhak, dhak,* as if someone was digging a well inside his heart. Rocks, sand, and pieces of sharp stone seemed to surround him. Tears streamed down his cheeks.

Rahmat Pathan did indeed come that evening. He brought three other Pathans with him. They stood outside the gate, and he entered the courtyard alone. "Parasu, Parasu!" he called out in a loud voice.

Sailabala came out, the end of her saree pulled low over her head, a stool in her hand. Seeing the huge figure of the man in front of her, she involuntarily drew back a couple of steps. Truly, in his white turban, black waistcoat and *Pathani* suit, Rahmat Pathan looked like the *Burha Dangoria* himself, that legendary angelic old ghost, who looked down benevolently upon the villages from the tops of the great banyan trees!

"I have not come here to sit," said the Pathan. "I want Parasu."

Parasu came out, "Have mercy, Pathan sir, have mercy," he pleaded.

"What's wrong?" asked the Kabuliwala.

"My brother is critically ill sir. The doctors can do nothing more in Guwahati, and we must take him to Vellore. I took the contract for the well hoping that I would be able to afford my brother's treatment. But it is useless — it could not help us."

Rahmat stood still for some time. Then he remarked, "Oh, yes. I was told that someone was taking chemotherapy. Was that your brother?"

"Yes", replied Parasu.

"Then that terrible incurable disease will..." Again he stopped. "I would like to see the boy," he said. "Would you mind us Muslims entering your house to see him?"

"Of course not, sir," said Parasu

Rahmat Pathan took off his turban, and stooping, entered the small doorway, just managing to avoid hitting the upper frame. In the dim light of the oil lamp, he saw Damodar sitting on the bed, looking more like a skeleton than a living man. His big eyes in his sunken cheeks shone in the lamplight as though they were two flickering, fading lamps in a deep, dark tunnel. His head with its dry stubble of hair looked too big for his emaciated body. Rahmat Pathan stood staring silently and intently at his face for some time. Then he looked at the boy's arms and legs.

Raising his hands high above his head, he appeared to be saying something to the boy. Then he came outside, and looking up at the heavens, he stretched out his hands.

Parasu and his mother watched him perplexed. What was the Pathan doing?

Rahmat took a handkerchief from his pocket— the same handkerchief in which Sailabala's earrings were tied. He handed it to Parasu and said, "Here, take it. And listen, you do not have to repay my debt just now. Take your brother for the best treatment. Don't you know that brothers are gifts from God? It is only through great good deeds that one gets a brother. Go and give him the best medical treatment possible..."

So saying, Rahmat Pathan left them, and cycled back the way he had come. The three other Pathans who had accompanied him followed hastily.

*The real character of pathan*

# THE EMPTY BOX

Most people are usually asleep at this hour. Even those homeless beggars who had recently come and settled in the vicinity of the graveyard did not get up so early in the morning.

Some *bulbuli* birds had just begun to stir and chirp in the branches of the *'hizol'* tree in front of Toradoi's shack, and a few moments ago, a line of small yellow-beaked cranes had flown noisily across the eastern horizon over the Brahmaputra River. An odd odour, created by the mixture of the stench of burnt flesh and the fresh fragrance of the small *kagzi* lemon flowers, blowing in from somewhere, filled the area.

Toradoi walked out of her hovel, and saw that Haibor, the man who sold firewood for burning the dead, was standing beneath the tree as usual. In the faint light of this early dawn, his thin legs protruding from the black half pants he wore stood out distinctly, and his white teeth shone out like pieces of chewed sugarcane.

She mumbled with displeasure on seeing him, and rushed back indoors. What did she have, to make him stand there day in and day out, waiting as if to suck out her very bones? Some of the things he had said to her rang anew in her ears. – "That drunken driver of yours will not be out from jail for a long time yet. And who knows whether he will be released at all? After all, he has knocked down and killed not one but two persons, and it has been proved that he was drunk when he was driving. But do not worry, I will help you. Keep your door open one night, just one night, and your two boys will not have to starve any more."

It was this hope of seeing her door open some night that motivated Haibor to stand beneath the *hizol* tree every morning, long before the hour other people woke up, when only the small birds sat on the branches, chirping noisily among themselves.

After a little while Toradoi walked out again and looked around. The man in the half pants was no longer standing there. There were some people who had come furtively to see the wooden box she had picked up from the graveyard, but that Haibor, who supplied firewood for burning the dead was not among them.

She peeped out to see whether someone was still loitering around, trying to get a glimpse of the box. What kind of people were these, she thought to herself. They were more like starving dogs that smelled each other's bodies, trying to find out what they had eaten. They would not hesitate to snatch the very clothes off one's back and leave one naked. When the Zamindar of Chok Road died a few days back, his body was carried to the graveyard in his bed made of the most expensive wood. And now Haladhar chowkidar slept in that same bed with his ugly wife. And that Sukura's wife, who earned her living chopping wood, now used the fine *hookah* she had picked up in the graveyard to smoke her tobacco. Someone had even found two gold rings lying among the charred remains of a well-to-do dead person! But no one had bothered to go and see those things. No one had been interested to go and see how the poverty-stricken Haladhar's hideous wife slept on the expensive wooden bed.

The hovels, sheds, shacks and flimsy shelters of all types, made out of old corrugated sheets, etc., that had sprung up in the areas around the cemetery, were full of such possessions left by the relatives of the rich dead who were cremated there. Many luxurious and showy objects that had once been the pride and joy of some well-to-do family, now lay incongruously in the hut of some penniless beggar, grinning maliciously at its own social comedown! But there was no curiosity about these things. It seemed that these nasty people were intent only in maligning her with her black box. Toradoi went inside again, and glanced at her two sons. They were sleeping soundly Both of them were pitifully thin — their rib cages were so prominent that one could count their ribs. Their tattered half pants hung down from their bloated lower abdomens, -looking very much like the dried up skin of the goats slung up in a butcher's shop. And there, near them, was that wooden box. A youth seemed to stand inside it, the personification of a restless youthful strength !

Toradoi touched the beautiful flowers that were carved into the wood, and the lovely *bakul* flowers seemed to take on life and become real flowers. She put her head down on the box and caressed the flowers with her cheeks. Then, she climbed into the open box, and as she had on every other night since she had brought it into her hut, she lay down inside it.

An unusual sensation of happiness flowed over her, and under its overwhelming spell, she lay inside that large box for a long time — that coffin that someone had left behind after burning the dead body that had been inside it. When she had picked that box up from the graveyard, she had found some pieces of blood stained ice that had been inside it. But she did not seem to remember that now. Toradoi could be heard sobbing inside the box.

After some time a police vehicle drove noisily past her shack. Indeed, the only cars that passed this way were the police vehicles. They came to make enquiries about some things — like whether the "handing over certificates" of the person killed in some firing incident were in order, or whether it was true that some one had come surreptitiously and buried an illegal baby, without any certificate from the hospital, and so on and so forth.

Also, the business of the Satgaon prostitutes was flourishing here; as if the more human flesh that was burnt, the hotter grew their own flesh and animal instincts. Besides, there were so many unregistered corpses that were brought here to be cremated... These, and so many other such matters made the police vehicles come almost daily to this graveyard. They came and discussed the issue, and quarrelled with the members of the "*shamshaan* committee". Then they left.

Hearing the sound of the police Jonga jeep, Toradoi sat up inside the coffin. How had she become so emotionally entangled in the box, she wondered? There ...there were so many things, so many thoughts! Dear God, the box was strewn with vermilion, and flowers. Last night, she had brought out the blouse she had worn on her wedding day, and put it on. It was the only piece of clothing she still had that was not tattered and torn. Then in the dim light of the kerosene lamp, she had stood before her small mirror and carefully combed her hair — as carefully and eagerly as she had done on her wedding day ten years ago. As she combed her hair almost passionately, she hardly noticed that the comb often scratched the bones on her shoulders and her neck. In the days gone by, when her body was covered with soft, healthy flesh, she had not even known that there were any bones in these places. Now, people said, that since she had come to live among the skeletons in the graveyard, she herself had turned into a skeleton.

This wooden box was really marvellous. Lying inside it, Toradoi felt as though she was sleeping with the lover she desired so passionately. Her hair, her hair oil and vermilion, all these were distinctly marked inside this box.

Could someone still be peeping inside to see what she was doing with the black box? Many people had been trying to see the box, and what she was doing with it, trying to look through cracks in the door and the window and through the thin walls. She suspected that they were even telling her two boys to keep a watch on her and her actions.

'Oh, how horrible!' , they seemed to be saying. 'How could anyone sleep inside a coffin? ! Throw it away, get rid of it!' Toradoi lay down inside the box again, and that feeling overwhelmed her — that unique sensation — something she had never felt before!

Suddenly there was the sound of someone kicking heavily on her door and Toradoi jumped out of the box in alarm. She listened intently, and knew that it was her brother, Someswar, who worked in the police force.

"Toradoi, Toradoi!" he called out. And as soon as she opened the door, a big man dressed in police uniform walked in. He was a large, robust man, sporting a huge moustache, wearing a pair of rough boots, and carrying a stout stick in his hand. Without any explanation, he marched into the room. He said, "I have not been able to come and see you. But today I have been put on duty here, so I could come. It seems that that loose woman from Satgaon has opened a veritable office here! It is really scandalous, the way things are going! Religion and decency have disappeared. When Barua died the other day, his two sons came to this graveyard carrying their dead father. But while one of them, dressed only in a 'gamocha' was busy with the rituals for his dead father, the other one suddenly disappeared from the scene. He sneaked away to that prostitute's room without any of the others even being aware of it! These are the times we are living in!" Suddenly he stopped talking and stared in front of him. Then he jumped back as though he had seen a poisonous snake. He stared in shocked surprise at the big black box in front of him.

Then coming close to it he knocked on its wood with his stick. He even walked around it attentively, as though he was carrying out the ritualistic *"pradakshin"*. Then, kneeling down near it, he took out a handkerchief from his pocket and wiped his face. The man who had walked into the room in such a careless and pompous manner now looked like a defeated soldier. Glancing towards Toradoi, he asked in a small voice, "Do you have any water in the house? Give me a glass of water, then."

He gulped the water down at one go. Then with his head bent, he said, "So, what I thought was right. This is that box. Yes, yes, it is the same coffin." Suddenly, lifting his head and looking straight at her he said, "You worked in their house as their maid servant. When the young man's father, Thakur, lay ill, you helped them greatly, even washing his soiled clothes .Everyone knows that. And the son?"

Now this big and sturdy constable almost broke down weeping. He spoke in a broken and emotional voice, "The young man had an affair with you, did he not? At that time he said he was determined to marry you. And the entire Thakur household was in a great turmoil over this. Ultimately came his transfer to Upper Assam — and then this accident."

Without any preamble, Toradoi suddenly asked him a question, "What hit him?"

"A jeep," Someswar replied. "What a handsome man he was! I removed the bloodstained pieces of ice with my own hands, and helped to put his body on the funeral pyre. A young man's blood! These two hands of mine were absolutely..."

Seeing Toradoi standing there stiffly like a statue, he could not finish the sentence. The big black box stood between them like a mysterious cavern...

Someswar stood up, and in a rather dramatic manner, he

shouted, "The days when a tea garden *sahib* could marry Toradoi, the daughter of a *coolie* are long past. That Jenkins *Sahib*, who dared to marry a *coolie* labourer's daughter died a long time ago. That big man's younger son Saru Bopai said he would marry you, that he loved you with all his heart. But could he marry you? Could he take you out from this hovel and give you a place in their grand bungalow?"

Toradoi cried out in a heartbroken voice, "Twelve years have gone by since that time. He did not marry all these years because he could not marry me. Maybe he would not have married at all if he had lived."

The big, bossy constable stared at her as if he could not believe his ears. Then he started scolding her and accusing her.

"You fool!" he scolded, "You were foolish enough to give everything a woman holds most dear all those years ago, and you still have not learnt anything. You are still a big fool. I am a policeman, and when I heard what you had done, I came prepared."

Toradoi gazed helplessly at her elder brother. "What is he saying? Dear God, what is he trying to say now? "she cried.

Someswar continued, "Now, even after losing everything else, that man is trying to rob you of that which you have so long carried around with you as your most precious possession."

In the meantime, the two boys had woken up, and the three of them stared at Someswar.

" O God! , what is he thinking of now?" thought Toradoi. "What is he trying to say?"

The poverty-stricken mother and her two starving sons

looked like three ghostly spirits of the cemetery, as they gazed at the well-fed man in front of them.

Someswar felt around in his pockets , and the two small boys thought that their uncle was about to give them some money — like other visitors often gave them — like the man always waiting under the *hizol* tree pushed coins into their hands when no one was looking. This man was their own uncle, their mother's brother but he had not come to visit them even when their father was taken to the prison.

Someswar got up and taking out a bundle of letters from his pocket threw them in Toradoi's face. He said, "These are the invitation cards for his wedding. As I said, I came prepared when I heard about your doings. See, he was not waiting for you, vowing to marry no one but you. His wedding date was fixed, and even the invitation cards were printed. Read them, read these invitation letters. He was on his way home for his wedding when the accident took place... Read these letters, and pray for the peace of his departed soul."

As he was stamping out of the room, his glance fell on Toradoi's two sons, who were now holding on closely to her. Muttering to himself, he put his hands inside his trouser pockets looking for coins to give them.

If he could have caught that loose woman who carried on her trade even with persons who came to cremate their dead, he might have been able to make some money; or even if he could have caught that Haibor red-handed! That scoundrel sold cheap wood and passed it off as the more expensive *sal,* to the mourners coming to burn their dead!

Finding some loose coins, he handed a fistful of them to his small nephews, then walked quickly out of the door. The two half starved boys, finding money in their hands, bolted out to the small shop.

Toradoi sat near the bundle of invitation letters. She felt them with her hands — like the sons of the dead felt about in the ashes of the funeral pyre for the '*Asthi*' (the remains of their bones). There was no doubt that these were indeed invitation letters.

For a long time after this, Toradoi did not come out of her hut. Unable to bear the pangs of hunger, her two sons started to beg for food from the people who came to the graveyard to cremate their dead. Someone had even tied a *gamocha* around the younger boy's head — probably a *gamocha* someone had worn while performing the last rituals. The boys had picked up two liquor bottles from the top of a heap of firewood and washed them. There was a well near the statue of Yama Devta riding on a buffalo. The boys scooped up water from this well in their bottles, and drank that. The neighbours came to know what was happening. They knew that Toradoi did not bother to cook these days. She just sat in front of that huge box with its lid wide open, just like the open mouth of hell!

Haibor continued to wait for her beneath that tree every day.

Very early one morning, Toradoi and her sons were seen dragging the coffin out towards the graveyard. They dragged it to the place where, it was rumoured, someone had burnt an illegal baby, without any "handing over" certificate from the hospital. There Toradoi burnt the box.

The small *bulbuli* birds woke up and started their noisy start to the day. A bright red sun rose over the Brahmaputra River. The sun was surrounded by yellowish and light brown clouds. It was not like an ordinary sun — it was more like the flushed face of a helpless prostitute — a face distorted with the fear and slander of having to spend a night with an unwanted man. The light coloured clouds seemed to lay bare the helplessness of that face, and at the same time, the readiness of the face to fight against her destiny.

The ashes of the burnt box lay scattered all around the graveyard, looking like the skin of a freshly slaughtered goat , spread out to dry in the morning sunlight.

The noise of the *bulbuli* birds on the branches of the *hizol* tree increased to a fever pitch.

Toradoi came out of her hut. No *chador* covered her body.

The surprising thing was that the man who always stood waiting for her beneath the tree was not there that day..

Toradoi walked further down. But the man was not there...

# A City In Its Nakedness

Urmila Bhttacharjee's friends cried out in surprise when they saw the boy standing in a corner of the huge room. "He looks like a ghost, a spirit!"

"Where did you get him from?" they asked in amazed disbelief. The subject of all this speculation however was completely unaffected by all this.

The famous journalist who was in the group of her friends said, "So when you went out yesterday, you did some real social service!"

"How did you come to know about my going?" Urmila asked him.

"Yesterday, in the coffee house, you introduced Krishna Kapur to Dr.Ismaili, and you had told them that you wanted to go to the slums with them and their students."

She nodded, and replied gravely, "It seems that more than twenty five per cent of India's population comprises of Harijans.

And I firmly believe that each one of us should go out and try to do whatever little we can to help them. See, Mr.Rupchandra, you are always complaining that there are many people who talk about social service, but there are very few who actually go out and do anything .But just you wait and see! I will keep this boy and teach him to read and write, and make a useful man out of him."

"You say you want to make a man out of him?" said Professor Thakur. " But see that you do not shirk your duties for that. You must give your full time to your profession."

Urmila smiled, " Oh, you do not have to worry about that," she said. "You will see that after a couple of days, he will be the one to help us out in some things — like bringing *'meethapaan'* and cigarettes for all of us!"

Rupchandra could not contain his natural journalistic curiosity. " Now tell us, where did you find this 'thing'? Your penchant for describing things in detail is well known! So, …"

"I had got a sort of stimulus, or motivation you may say, to do something like this a long time ago. At that time my father was the headmaster of a school, and one day after coming back from playing with my friends, I found my father's friend, the Deputy Inspector of Schools sitting with him in our living room. Our small servant boy, Lakhan, was sitting in a corner scribbling something with a piece of charcoal. I was the apple of my father's eye, and as soon as I entered I went to him and hugged him. I said to him, "Look father, look at that Lakhan! He does not even know how to write his name! He is just sitting there struggling to write!"

Taufik Hussain looked up at me and said, 'Come here, my child. You just said that the servant boy can't even write his name, didn't you? Do you know, that this is your fault my dear girl."

I was astounded. How was I to blame for it? Hussain explained. And although at that time — I must have been about fourteen years old — I could not really understand what he was trying to tell me but I never forgot his words."

"I am sure that you are aware that nowadays it is illegal to keep young children in one's house," said Rupchandra.

The professor replied that this law should be changed, and asked her where she had found the boy.

"Yesterday I went with Krishna of the English department, to do some social work in the slums in Okhla. I think some of you know that these days I sometimes feel a bit afraid to stay alone in my house in my leisure time. In fact, I have sometimes even thought of drinking in order to ward off my loneliness. Anyway, yesterday, after the boys and girls had gone home, Krishna and I went and sat in a *dhaba* nearby and ordered two cups of tea. It was a *dhaba* that is frequented by the drivers of the trucks that go to and fro from Haryana. As we sat on one of the wooden benches sipping our tea, a woman who looked more like a ghost or an evil spirit than a human being came and stood in front of us. In fact I feel sort of ashamed to call her a woman.

"In places like Janakpuri and around the Nizamuddin station, or travelling on a double decker bus along the Gurudwara road, one can always see these beings, more lumps of flesh than anything else," continued Urmila. "But the apparition that appeared in front of us was something quite different."

"Different in what way?" asked the journalist. Urmila looked up at him. "She had a very peculiar appearance," she replied. "Her hands and feet were thin like dry sticks. But she had a huge ugly stomach that protruded in the front like a sack of jaggery. There was no flesh anywhere else on her body, except that vulgar stomach. And that was not all. She had two more kids with her, who were emaciated and starving and looked like ghosts. She came near us and started wailing and snivelling. 'Their father was a driver in the Haryana Roadways. One day he knocked down a man in Roshanara, and has not been seen ever since then. Please help me with some money'

"You want money, alms?" Krishna snapped at her.

"But how can you blame her Krishna? Don't all the *pundits* go around shouting that there is nothing more loathsome and shameful than begging? And educated people like us should not encourage begging by giving money to whoever asks for it? But when a ghost like creature appears suddenly before you, what can you do? Those awful unnaturally bright eyes! That sack like stomach...

"I stared at her for some time," Urmila continued. "In the meantime she had gone and sat down on one of the benches. Her ugly nose was sweating, and she started sobbing. On any other day, the owner of the *dhaba* would probably have chased her out like a dirty and sick dog. But for some reason, at that moment no one seemed to want to go near her or chase her away. Human sympathy is indeed rare in this concrete jungle of ours, where the people are usually selfish and cruel. But even here, at times, certain scenes render the people speechless. She presented just such a scene!"

"What happened then?" asked the reporter Rupchandra.

Urmila replied, "She stopped sobbing and looking at the two of us she said, 'You carry books in your hands and have bags on your shoulders. So you must be teachers. Take this boy of mine and teach him to at least write his name. You are educated people so I am sure you will not mind taking water from a Harijan's hands. I remember the man dressed in Khadi clothes, who came to teach us the *Rashtrabhasha* did not mind taking water from my hands. Take the boy, he will at least be able to heat the water for your baths.' When they heard these words, the owner of the *dhaba* and his workers burst out laughing. The woman jumped up in anger and snapped at them like a dog that had been hurt. 'I feel ashamed to call you men!' she screamed. 'Don't you have sisters and mothers? Suppose they were burdened like me with a stomach like a sack of salt? What would you have done then? You are not men. You never can be true men!' She started sobbing again.

"For a while, no one spoke. Then I said, 'All right, give me the boy. I will take him, and if I can do nothing else, I can at least teach him our *Rashtrabhasha*. Then he will be able to go to the camp in Kingsway and sit for the examinations there.' Krishna jumped up in shock! 'What are you doing?' she said. 'Don't you know how dangerous it is to pick up urchins from the roads in Delhi? Have you forgotten how that teacher of Nizamuddin was murdered?'

"But I was not in a mood to listen to Krishna at that time. I went forward and caught hold of the boy's hands, but he tried to hide behind his mother. I saw then that he was not a young child as I had earlier thought. The owner of the *dhaba*, a tough and stalwart Punjabi fellow, said, 'There is a police station nearby. Take them there and do the matter in an official way. Do not just pick up boys like this one from the streets.'

"As soon as she heard the word police, the woman said, "The white *sahibs* took pity on us Harijans. They taught my man to drive. But he went and knocked a man down and fled. The police came to the *jhuggi* three times to find him.'

"The *dhaba* owner yelled at her to go away. 'Don't listen to her,' he said. Well after that I brought the boy here. That is another story."

Rupchandra and Professor Thakur looked at the boy again.

Rupchandra said, "In Kolkata alone there are more than one lakh and twenty thousand people who sleep on the footpaths. Have you read any Dalit literature?"

Thakur shook his head.

"Urmila, I don't think you have read the works of the Dalit poets, Narayan Survey, Arun, and Namdeo Dhasla. They are now dreaming dreams of the rising sun. That is why one Dalit poet has written :-

"How will they stop minds
gone ablaze?
No more reasoning now,
Unreason helps a lot once the horizon is red.
What's wrong in keeping doors open?"

Professor Thakur and the journalist Rupchandra sat there talking till late into the night.

Neither of the three — Professor Thakur, Rupchandra nor Urmila, had happy or satisfactory lives. People said that the beautiful woman who worked in the 'Srinivas Mills' was too good for the thin and emaciated journalist. She had been fair and her body had been soft and lovely, like a blooming flower. But after she had gone to live in the '*barsati*' in Paharganj, and in Miani, the harsh sun of Delhi had burnt her beautiful soft body black. And the dry winds of March had played havoc with her silky shampooed hair. Ah! the poor journalist.

Professor Thakur lived with his wife and two children in two small cramped rooms in a '*barsati*' in Roshanara Road. He also had to send money regularly to his parents. Ever since the old owner of the house died, the new owner had been urging him to vacate the '*barsati*', because apparently he wanted to demolish the house and build a new one. Professor Thakur could not afford to go to an agent to find a new place to live in. So he had wandered around Delhi looking for a place. If, in these wanderings, he happened by chance to sit near Urmila, he would be filled with a sense of happy fulfilment. At such times, he would feel as though the dreams he had dreamt when he had passed out from Lucknow University with a First Class First position, were bearing fruit and blossoming into a sheltering tree! And he would sit there with Urmila, bemused with happiness.

He invariably had to face a class of unruly, uninterested, and insolent students, some of whom sat smoking openly. Yet, he mused, the students had, just a few years back listened to his lectures with avid interest, and had discussed and even argued with him about difficulties of Camu's philosophy. But the present generation of students were callous and never discussed anything with him. They seemed to ignore his very existence! One day, the professor tripped on a beer bottle at the door of the classroom. He was told that the students had taken to drinking because of their frustration, anxiety, and desire to be 'in' with their peer groups!

It was only three years since Urmila had come to live in Delhi, after being selected as a lecturer in the Hindi department of Delhi University. She was yet to complete her probationary period. A terrible incident had completely upset her smooth life. Her husband who worked in the English Department in the same University had gone abroad for higher studies, and had not returned. Some of their friends who had returned from the same place after completing their studies, had spread a sordid story about her husband's affair with a French woman. Urmila had built up a beautiful and happy life with her husband, and after this frightful incident, she had been completely broken. She spent her days unhappily, staying with her various brothers and sisters. Her parents had died long ago.

Finally, after finishing her studies, she had managed to land this job in the Delhi University.

After having to face a lot of bitter experiences, Urmila finally came to the conclusion that she must build her broken and tragic life anew. Her mind had become like a hunter's mind, searching all the time for her beloved in every man she met.

As they sat together, Rupchandra waited — almost willed, for Professor Thakur to go away and leave him alone with Urmila, and Thakur thought that the journalist would leave. But neither of them left. The two men indeed were friends, but at such moments they became the worst of enemies! They sat there until about half past eight, talking about all sorts of things, from the *durbar* of King George the Fifth, to Jaspal, to Shamsher Bahadur's poetry. Ultimately both of them left together late in the night.

This was the Delhi of 1978. And the city had already earned the dubious title of being one of the most infamous and dangerous cities. So, after seeing her friends off, Urmila quickly went upstairs and locked her door.

She had not forgotten that she had promised to educate Jagannath, so one day she went to the Harijan school in the Kingsway camp taking the boy with her. She had hoped that the boy's mother would come to meet her son and enquire about his well being. But as time passed, Urmila gave up that hope.

Urmila knew the *Rastrabhasha* teacher of the school, the Hindi scholar Vishnu Prabhakar. Prabhakar was pleased to meet the boy and was all praise for Urmila.

"You are doing a very good thing. This is exactly what we want from educated ladies like you. Only the other day, our Prime Minister went to the Harijan Mahasabha and said that he was prepared to join their '*satyagraha*', demanding the fulfilment of their demands."

He told her that he would teach him twice a week, and asked her to get his books and other necessities ready. Jagannath started his studies in due course and proved to be an attentive and sincere student. Vishnu Prabhakar came regularly twice every week, and Urmila too tutored him with single minded enthusiasm whenever she had any free time. No one, not even his mother, came to see him for more than a month, but Urmila was not unhappy about this although she thought it rather strange.

After some time the Professor said to her, "Do you know, I truly think that after all you will succeed in your efforts to make a good man out of this boy you picked up from the slums. We ourselves are not always aware of the strengths that lie hidden inside our frail bodies and minds!"

Urmila tried to make a joke of this, and replied, "It takes a long time to find and  recognize the gold that lies hidden among the dust of the roads! When the boy comes to know us well, he might even resent your coming to visit me like this!"

The professor gazed at Urmila with a deep gravity that needed no further explanation. The deep emotional look they exchanged seemed to touch some deep chord in their hearts and took its roots there.

One day, some time later, Urmila came home from her classes to find the boy's mother sitting near the doorstep. She almost cried out, "Where were you all this time? Why did you not come to see him? Is he not your son, your flesh and blood?"

"Of course he is, *Memsahib*," she replied.

"So, have you come to take him back today?"

"No, why should I take him back, *memsahib*?"

Urmila was relieved to hear this. She noticed that the woman had changed quite a bit within the last six months. Her clothes were still in tatters, but they were clean. Also, there was no sign of the wildness and turmoil of that day. Her stomach too had become normal, she had probably given birth to a child in the meantime.

"Has Jagannath's father come back?" she asked the woman. She shook her head.

"Then where do you live now?" Urmila asked.

"There is some construction work going on in the Minto bridge. I work there under a contractor," she replied.

Then, like a very busy person, she said, "I have no time to waste.I have come to ask you if there are any old clothes you can give me. Besides, I also need some money."

The woman left, and Jagannath too went with her on his way to the milk booth. Urmila went up to the roof, and from there she saw that the woman was trying to show Jagannath the tattered state of the clothes she was wearing, trying probably to make him realize that she was still living in penury.

Jagannath returned in due course, and he got busy preparing tea and snacks. When they were sitting together having their tea, he said, "Those guests of yours will be coming soon. Would you teach me for some time before they arrive?"

They sat with their books under the clear sky, and Urmila was entranced by the surroundings — the pigeons roosting on the television wires, the bats flying in from the Roshanara gardens and almost covering the sky above her head like a dark cloud. She suddenly heard the sound of someone banging on the door. Jagannath went and opened the door. Urmila's old friend,

Jasowant, who was engaged in research work in mathematics, stood at the doorstep. At one time, there had been a deep relationship between them, and Urmila had been so deeply affected by it that she had even dreamed that she would be able to build her ruined life anew with him.

She had met him in the Arts faculty. He had told her that they were refugees from Lahore. She remembered that it was the month of April when she had first met him — the month when the beautiful Gulmohar trees were in full blooom in Delhi. Once, when she had been quite late after presenting a paper at a seminar in the Lady Sriram College, she had stood alone on the road. The bus service had become infrequent, and she thought that she would have to take a 'lift.' Many people who were stranded like this, she knew, often took a lift in the cars of strangers. She had also heard of many stories, both romantic and hair raising, about what sometimes happened to girls who had taken such lifts. But waiting alone on the streets of Delhi so late in the evening, Urmila was filled with a sense of unknown fear.

A Fiat passed by and she lifted her hand. But it did not stop. After a while she saw another car coming, and with some hesitation raised her hand once again. This time the car came to a halt very near her. The driver, wearing black framed glasses and with neatly combed hair, was obviously a gentleman. He opened the front door for her and asked her where she wanted to go.

"Mall Road," she replied.

"Where is your home?" he asked. "Who lives with you?" She did not like these questions. She was well aware of the atmosphere of the city, especially at a time like this and of the thoughts and feelings of men. Everything, every human feeling, seemed to have dried up and become hard and callous. At this moment, she thought, the minds of all men had become like the setting sun.

The car proceeded along the almost deserted road and crossed the crowded area of the ITO and India Gate. Suddenly the driver turned his eyes towards Urmila and gazed covetously at her bare arm, shining with perspiration. Urmila thought it best to get down here, in spite of the fact that it would not be easy to get on to a bus in this crowded place.

Sensing her indecision and hesitation, he said, "Madam?"

"Yes, yes, stop here," she said. By this time her body was glistening with sweat and her blouse was almost soaking wet.

" Are you sure you want me to drop you here?" he asked.

She nodded, "Yes."

"But..."

"But what?" she said. And as soon as he had braked she jumped out of the car.

The unknown man had probably got down from his car too and he followed her for some distance, because she heard his voice calling out to her — indeed chasing her... She stood near Maharana Pratap's statue for some time, trying to calm herself and catch her breath. She glanced back and saw that the car was no longer chasing her. There was nothing to fear!

When she came and stood at the bus shelter, she saw, among the three or four people there, the figure of the man she had seen so frequently for the past two years in the Arts Faculty, in the coffee house, on the research floor. How they introduced themselves was almost dramatic! He eagerly agreed to accompany her to her home. They got on to the bus together, and, like an old friend he said in a light-hearted manner, "When you get down from the bus at your stop you have to pass a rather frightening restaurant, don't you?"

"Will you believe me when I say that until now I have not looked up to see what there is on the road?"

" It is that Brahma restaurant where the conspiracy to kill Pratap Singh Kairon was hatched and planned!"

Urmila almost shouted in shock, " But I go past it every single day!"

After this, quite an intimate relationship grew between them. They were seen together everywhere — in the library, the coffee house, the seminar hall, the research floor, the International Centre etc.

Once when they were discussing marriage he said, "According to the Christian belief, some people are born impotent, and some are made impotent by other men. You can understand this in any way you like." And he had laughed out aloud! He must have been more than thirty years' old at that time. He still had the responsibility of marrying off two sisters and providing them with dowry. She wondered if that was what he meant.

After knowing him for two long years, Urmila came to a certain conclusion. She decided that Jasowant was the only man who could create a new world for her in place of the life that had been ruined by her errant husband. She waited for him to say what she wanted to hear from him — that he wanted to marry her and set up a family. But this hope gradually turned to disappointment and she had to force herself to stop seeing Jasowant. So when he suddenly appeared at her doorstep she was, for a moment at least, somewhat unsure and taken aback. But soon this was washed away by a wave of hope and happiness.

"Why are you standing out there?" she asked. "Come inside."

"First give me a cup of tea," he said. I have come on my scooter all the way from Defence Colony, via Palace Cinema and Roshanara Road. And let me tell you I feel as though I have just come out victorious from a particularly ferocious war!"

Urmila and Jagannath went inside to make tea and snacks. As they sat facing each other, sipping tea, Urmila noticed that Jasowant looked somewhat preoccupied. Was he about to say something, she wondered?

Without warning, she got up and going to the door yelled to Jagannath not to disturb them or knock at the door as they were busy with some important talk.

Jasowant gazed at Urmila while taking his tea. He looked at her face, her beautiful hair and soft, full body. But he noticed that the corners of her eyes were marked by a few lines that were a testimony to her sufferings and pain.

For a long time they sat there facing each other but not saying anything. The noises from the street gradually faded away, and they heard the sound of the shop shutters being closed down for the night. Urmila became a bit impatient. She thought to herself, 'Dear God, let my dreams of starting a new life bear fruit this day, or let me forget them forever.' The matter must be settled one way or the other today!

After a somewhat lengthy silence, he said, "It has been a long time since we have known each other."

She made no reply, and he continued, "Can we not come closer? Can we not have a more intimate relationship?"

Urmila looked sharply at him. "So," she said. "everything is clear now, isn't it? No matter how educated we women folk may be, no matter how empowered, our hearts yearn for protection, for support."

"Oh Urmila, Urmila," he protested. But today she had neither the time nor the inclination to listen to anything else.

When her extreme agitation had abated a little, her eyes filled with tears. Jasowant pulled his chair near hers and gently caressed her back.

"Listen to me Urmila. That was not what I came for." Urmila jumped up and took a step away from him. But he was not one to give up so easily either.

He advanced towards her. "Who told you that I would leave you and go away?" he asked. "No, I have no intention of going away. I want to make our relationship deeper than it is, put it on a firmer base."

"Make our relationship deeper and more firm!!" A part of her innermost being seemed to echo these words as she said them out loud! "But how do you propose to do so?" she asked.

Jasowant reared up like a ferocious beast! " Give me sex! You have to give me sex!" he almost shouted.

"Sex?"

"Yes, only sex can immortalize it."

She did not quite remember what had happened to her in that one brief moment. When after some time she opened her eyes, she saw that a glass vase lay crushed to bits on the floor near the table. She did not remember when Jagannath had come and cleaned up the scattered bits of broken glass. His hands had been cut by the glass pieces, but he did not seem to notice the blood on his hands.But when a little later the blood began to flow thicker and faster, Urmila saw it and like a woman gone mad, tore at her sari to make a bandage to stop the bleeding.Her wild eyes filled with tears, and she did not make any attempt to hide the tears from this young boy. At this moment this boy had become like a caring mother to her, and she found that she could cry her heart out in front of him without any embarrassment.

Her heart was filled with a sense of disgust for herself and a feeling of rebellion. But she managed to supress these feelings in front of this Harijan boy, who now seemed to become her only medium of expression, of support...

She called out to him, "Come Jagannath, come and make some coffee. We will sit on the balcony and have some coffee together. This is a very dirty world. But we will survive... Come and sit near me." They sat on the balcony sipping their coffee.

It was as though nothing unusual had just happened — as if it was simply another of the numerous accidents that occurred in Delhi every day! The Roshanara garden in the distance appeared dark at this time of the night, surrounded as it was by the bright lights of the streets around it.

Suddenly they heard someone shouting, "Madam, we are coming, open the door." The journalist and the professor climbed up the steps and entered the room.

There was another round of coffee. The three of them sat companionably chatting of various things. Seeing that Urmila seemed to be more animated than usual, neither of her two friends wanted to leave early. The Professor started talking about his early days.

"When Goyar was the Vice Chancellor," he started, "the entire atmosphere of Delhi University was different. After taking my interview, he pointed at another member of the Board and almost ordered, 'You will not bargain with him'."

This short-statured man had a fund of knowledge that was as deep as the sea itself. And this intellectualism, together with his simple, almost childlike innocence and gentleness, made a very attractive combination. Truly, that was an age that would never be seen again!

"It was the Science Congress of the year 1958. Eisenhower had come, so had the Duke of Edinburgh. A huge *pandal* had been constructed in the field opposite what is now the Registrar's office. Now that field has become the University playground. Do you remember the great ruckus that was created when both the Jansangi party supported by the DUTA and the Congress fought against each other to win the DUSU elections! The Communists simply sat there looking on, and could do nothing! But people say that during those terrible days during the Partition, it was the Communists who really helped the victims, often at the risk of their own lives.

"This 'language-less' Delhi was not always like this. The famous Mathurs from Mathura formed the intellectual group.

They understood the importance and value of learning, and scholars. Do you know where those famous 'Mushaiaras' were held?"

"Oh, those fragrant *attars* of Lucknow! Those *'paans'* which melted so soothingly as soon as you put them in your mouth! And those beautiful women of the Mathur clan — their fine poetry and love of the fine arts!"

Rupchandra became more and more excited, "Oh, those beautiful chiffon saris embroidered in golden *zari* work, the diamond nose tops, and the silver *'paandaans'*!

"Indeed, where have those days gone, those wonderful, graceful days!" echoed the professor nostalgically. "The fragrance of the *attars* has been taken over by the filthy smell of corrupt politics."

Even the shops that were still open were now closed with loud clattering sounds. The night *chowkidars* could be heard making their rounds banging their stout sticks on the roads to make it known that they were on duty. And then, gradually, the street became as silent as a graveyard.

But neither of Urmila's two guests showed any signs of leaving. Each seemed to be waiting for the other to leave first. Thakur started to get a bit impatient. He was a family man, and he felt that his wife had lately begun to be a bit suspicious. He worried that she might even send someone to Urmila's place looking for him. He knew that she was getting more annoyed with him. "Instead of spending your leisure time with that woman living there all alone, why don't you spend at least some evenings with your children looking after their school work?" she scolded.

"I was telling you about Maurice Goyer, wasn't I?" he said. "The then Vice Chancellor of Delhi University, Maurice Goyer, worked as an honorary officer refusing any salary. He was a saintly person if ever there was one. And his daughter Miranda..."

"You were telling us about the '*shamiana*' that had been erected in front of the 'old establishment', remember?" said Rupchandra.

"Yes, of course. VKRV Rao was the Treasurer at that time. The Duke of Edinburgh and Eisenhower had come as guests. Ah, those were the times! Can you ask that boy of yours to get us another round of coffee?"

Rupchandra was not pleased. He was at this moment longing to spend some time alone with Urmila.

For the first time since she had known them, Urmila found the two men to be both ugly and distasteful. They seemed like two hostile vultures sitting waiting for her — as though she was a lump of raw, naked flesh! Ugh! She almost yelled to Jagannath to quickly get more coffee.

Thakur began to speak with renewed enthusiasm. "I used to live in Hudson road at that time," he started. But Rupchandra interrupted, "What! In that infamous Hudson Road, that terrible frightening road!"

"Yes, yes, that cruel General Hudson after whom the road was named. He was the one who had arrested Bahadur Shah, the last emperor of *Bharat*. You have heard of the 'Khooni *Darwaza*' near Dilli Gate, haven't you? The dying emperor had been invited to come to that place telling him that some understanding would be arrived at during the meeting.

The aged king had come in a camel drawn covered carriage with hope in his heart. He had come from the Red Fort to where the Maulana Azad Medical College is located now. At this point, that wicked General Hudson had sent a gift to the Emperor, a gift on a golden plate covered with a silk *chador*. The dying Bahadur Shah removed the covering *chador*, and what did he find!"

Professor Thakur looked at the rapt and curious faces of Rupchandra and Urmila.

"Truly it was a hair -raising, and blood -curdling gift! It was the head of the Emperor's son!"

Both his listeners stared in shocked silence.

"Zaffar's tomb still lies in the house number fifty-eight in the bazaar in Rangoon. It seems that the bungalow was previously occupied by some English captain."

Fresh cups of coffee came, and with that the gossip started with renewed vigour. Once again the talks veered around to affairs of the University — to Edwina Mountbatten's wedding proposal, to the fact that the house was currently being used as the 'finance five' office etc.

"Have you had occasion to visit the 'Finance Five' recently?" asked the professor. "Have you seen that huge cat that jumps from one table to the next one during lunch hour?" All of them laughed out loud. But to Urmila the laugher seemed rather hysterical. Neither Rupchandra nor the professor left until after ten o'clock that night.

Right around this time someone kicked violently at the

door. The door burst open, and Jagannath shot inside like a bullet. He stood in the centre of the room and pointing an accusing finger at Urmila he said, "Do you know that the shopkeepers down there speak badly about you? My mother spends her time eating and drinking tea with the contractors at the Development block. She does that out of sheer hunger. But you have no hunger in your stomach. Why do you spend half the night with these wicked and selfish men? Why? What difference is there between you and those 'bad' women living in the slums?"

What happened after this outburst is another story...

Jagannath went out. Urmila's two men friends did not give much importance to this incident. Only professor Thakur questioned, "What would you have done in the end? Think of the whole thing with foresight. He will be growing up, and soon he will be a young man, with all a young man's instincts. What will happen after that?"

Faced with this thought, Urmila too became confused and a bit scared.

Rupchandra too echoed the professor's thoughts. "Yes, ultimately, what would you have done? What would you, living in a house with mosaic floors, understand about the frightful conditions of the people living in slums?"

"Listen, I spent so much time in the slums of Turkman gates and other places that the soles of my shoes got worn out. I am very well acquainted with all the horrors of life in the slums. They are terrible and frightening areas. And dealing with a boy you randomly picked up from one of these places..."

Urmila listened helplessly to all they had to say. But in her heart of hearts she thought that Rupchandra, living as he claimed to have done for so long, among the rough horrors of the cruel city of Delhi, must surely have been influenced by the callousness and horrors of the city. Since the terror filled atmosphere of the city had affected ninety per cent of the population, why should these two be left out?

After Jagannath had left, Urmila was left with a strange feeling of loneliness. And in order to forget this loneliness she started spending more and more time in the Central Library. A few days later a couple of her fellow teachers reminded her that her probationary period would soon be over, and that she should meet the Head of the Department regarding it. So one day she made an appointment and went to meet the Head.

"You are Urmila Bhattacharjee?" he asked. "Have you ever participated in the departmental seminars?"

"Many times, Sir," she replied. He looked at her with raised eyebrows as if he found it hard to believe her.

"What are you working on?" he asked.

"On women in Ramayani literature," she replied

"But many others have already worked on this topic."

"That's true," she said. "But every researcher has his own ideas and concepts, that are usually quite different from those of others. Besides the injustices that were meted out to women in our country in those days are..." She saw that the Head had taken out some new files and stopped mid-sentence. Knowing that she would be wasting her time if she sat there, she quietly left the room.

It was the month of December and Delhi was continuously covered by a blanket of dust, and her hands and feet had become rough and dry. As she stood on the main street she wondered at herself. Until just some time ago, she had taken such a lot of care about her looks. She had used all kinds of creams and moisturizers to keep her face and body soft and smooth! But where had all that eagerness, that care for her looks disappeared? Now she dressed without bothering about her appearance; her shoes were old and almost worn out, her hair had lost its sheen and had become rough. She was gradually coming to a stage where she could hardly recognize herself!

She stood there on the road wondering where she could go. Then she got on to the bus going to Okhla.

Even as she sat among the crowd of passengers, she had a strange feeling that was one of a kind, different from everyone elses. She was scared of her extreme loneliness. All the time, one sentence of Jagannath echoed and re - echoed in her mind — "There is no difference between those bad women living in the slums and you."

By the time she changed buses at the Central Secretariat stop, Urmila felt as though she were going mad. When she was a child, she remembered, her father was afraid to let her cross the road by herself. And today! How many roads she had had to cross all by herself! Loneliness had followed her like an incurable disease.

She had written her name and address and kept it in her handbag, as a precaution she supposed. She got down from the bus and entered the awful slum area. A group of horrible looking people came and surrounded her. She had come at a time when the slum dwellers eyed all cleanly and decently dressed people with suspicion. They suspected that such persons might be spies. The people were afraid that even the ramshackle roofs covering their heads would be snatched away from them in order to make space for buildings.

After a little while, a thin old man came and took Urmila near a wooden door. He went inside and came out bringing a woman with him. Urmila was left in no doubt that the woman was Jagannath's mother.

Guilt and shame left Urmila speechless for a couple of minutes, although she could not understand why she should feel guilty.

The woman said, "You took my boy promising that you would educate him, didn't you? Well, will you come inside or stand out here?"

" No, its all right. I will not come in. Will he come back again?"

"How can I say whether he will go back? Tell me, is there any difference between your promises and those of a drunken man?"

The thin old man cleared his throat and commented, "Making promises is a luxury with people like her." Probably frustration and a hard life had made the man so harsh, thought Urmila. Besides what else could he think after the boy had come away like that.

Again the woman said, "There is nowhere to sit inside."

Urmila was a bit upset. "I am aware that your present condition is very bad. The boy's father probably has not come back."

Apparently almost on the verge of tears, she replied, "After he left you he got into a gang of bad boys of the slum. This young boy has learnt to say that all the people in this world are bad. He says that those who we think are good are merely playing a role."

The sun set in the disturbed horizon far away. The tattered hutments of the slum looked as though a violent storm had blown across them.

"How long will you stand outside like this?" she asked.

"I will go now," replied Urmila. "Send him back if he wants to come. And tell him that my doors will always be open for him."

Before leaving, Urmila almost shouted at the woman, "I took him with me because I wanted to educate him, and make a man out of him. My promise was in no way a matter of luxury for me. I meant what I said, and I still stand by my word!"

It started raining. It was that out–of–season rain that makes people shiver in December. Opening the door one wet morning, Urmila found Jagannath waiting on the doorstep. He seemed to have aged in the last four months. His hair was scruffy, and his skin had become rough, and his clothes were in tatters. When he opened his mouth, it smelt of '*biri*', the cheap local cigarette. Urmila was sad and worried.

"What happened to you?" she asked. He did not reply. But the bundle under his arm reassured Urmila that he had come to stay. She realized that the barrier that had come up between this Harijan boy and herself in the last four months would be difficult to break down.

"So you have come back with the intention of continuing your studies?" she asked him. Again he made no reply.

"Where have you been staying all this time?" she persisted.

" In Nigambodh Ghat,"he said.

Urmila was struck as though by a bolt of lightning! Nigambodh Ghat! The only crematorium in the whole of India where a dead human body was cremated with no less than seven '*maunds*' of firewood!It was the only place where the entire body was burnt to ashes, leaving no half burnt pieces that had to be thrown into some river. It was in this place that the boy had spent four months in the company of a group of poverty stricken boys! She was appalled!

She wondered whether she should send him away. But then she would be all alone again. No, no, let him stay.

She felt as though she knew no one at all in this cruel city — her husband who had gone abroad for higher studies and disappeared, her siblings who had become completely absorbed in their own families and had no time for her, Rupchandra and Professor Thakur who professed to be her friends... and Jasowant? Her parents had been good, simple people, but they had passed away long ago.She had been brought up in an atmosphere of simple, but high culture. But now? No, let the boy stay and give her whatever company he could. Maybe after all, she had discovered a piece of gold amidst all the cruelty and callousness of this infamous city!

He went inside and washed. He went and kept his clothes tidily in the place where he used to stay before. Then looking around the house he sighed and said, "You seem to have forgotten to clean and tidy your house." Without further ado, and without asking her, he set about cleaning and dusting the rooms.

But the wall, the unseen and unacknowledged barrier that had grown between them remained as it was.

The out-of-season rain continued for three days and no one came to visit her during this time. She spent the days reading, and in the evenings she went out and sat on the balcony looking at the bats of the Roshanara garden, with their heavy black wings, flying about slowly, that to her depressed mind somehow resembled a sombre crematorium!

Sometimes Jgannath came and stood near her. He took care of all her needs — her lunch, her dinner and her tea. He remembered the timings. He also told her with great enthusiasm that this time he would really study hard and show everyone what he could do, He would startle everyone with his diligence!

On the fourth day after his arrival, he seemed somewhat impatient. The rain still poured down bringing life in the city almost to a standstill.

That evening, when the bats were just starting their daily flying routine, he strode into the balcony. In a harsh and rough voice he announced, "Our Harijan boys who live in the Nigambodh Ghat wanted to beat up that Vishnu Prabhakar who comes to teach us Hindi."

"Dear God!" exclaimed Urmila, " But why? What harm did the man do to you? He has been working virtually like a God among the illiterate youth there without a care for himself. Look at his worn out shoes, his old clothes! Is that not selfless service?"

Jagannath roared, "The boys whom he taught in Turkman Gate and Najaffgarh are now going around looking for jobs, with their certificates of passing the *Rashtrabhasha* exams. But they do not get any jobs. Those certificates are useless."

At this moment he looked quite ugly with his wide nostrils and his *biri-* stained black lips.

Urmila remained silent. What could she say? It seemed to her at this moment that he had suddenly become a fearsome man striding about menacingly in her balcony! Wonder of wonders!

Again he spoke, "You have been cooped up in your house alone all these days. No one has come to visit you. That is very bad, isn't it?"

What was he implying, this young boy, almost still a child! He was talking like an experienced man! Had his friends in Nigambodh Ghat taught him to talk like this, even to his elders? Sometime that evening he once again disappeared.

He did not return until very late that night, and Urmila became more and more agitated. She went up to the '*chhat*' (roof). It was still drizzling, and the street lights looked dim, like the cataract covered eyes of an old man. The bats from Roshanara gardens covered the sky looking like a blanket of dark clouds. The atmosphere was fearsome. She suddenly noticed two shadowy figures advancing towards her house. They were the only figures in that deserted street.

Urmila climbed down from the *chhat*. There was heavy knocking on her door. Opening the door, she cried out in shock! The mathematics research scholar Jasowant was standing at the door taking off his soaking raincoat. With him was Jagannath, his black lips reeking of the '*biri*'.

Jagannath came forward and said, "I had met Jasowant *sahib* as I was strolling around Nigambodh Ghat. I caught him and have brought him to you. He cannot escape... I told him that you have been sitting here all alone like a ghost. Now go inside and enjoy yourselves. You do not have to worry, I will sit here on the steps and guard you. Only, when your men friends leave, tell them to put some cash into the tin box I will be holding. I will always sit on these steps guarding you..."